1

# WATER UNDER THE BRIDGES

*A Local History and Chronicle
of the Life and Times of a Runcorn Family*

by

## FREDA PRICE

HORSESHOE PUBLICATIONS, WARRINGTON, CHESHIRE

© FREDA PRICE 1994
First published 1994

ISBN 1 899310 00 2

British Library Cataloguing in Publication Data.
A Catalogue record for this book is available from the
British Library.

Printed in Great Britain by
ANTONY ROWE LTD
CHIPPENHAM, WILTSHIRE

for the Publishers
HORSESHOE PUBLICATIONS
P.O. BOX 37, KINGSLEY
WARRINGTON
CHESHIRE WA6 8DR

Cover design and illustrations by TRACY WALKDEN

# LIST OF ILLUSTRATIONS

*Illustrations by Cheshire artist Tracy Walkden*

# CHAPTER 1

Runcorn, a Cheshire town on the south bank of the River Mersey, was my birthplace and later home for many of the changing scenes of my life. Its siting as a natural harbour at the river's edge initiated early local shipbuilding, but consequent development as a small port and thriving town was due chiefly to the cutting of the Bridgewater Canal through it - an artificial waterway which, together with its offshoots and connections, enabled industrial raw materials such as coal, salt and china clay to be carried conveniently within a wide area. To my maternal great-grandparents narrow boats on the canal (pulled by cart horses plodding at a leisurely pace along the towpaths without guidance) would have been a familiar sight.

In Cheshire the Bridgewater wound for miles through the lush fields, edged now and then with woods, which in summer were full of bluebells, red campions and foxgloves and were popular haunts for picnickers. Cattle grazed in the meadows and the water was clear except for the floating remains of a dead rat or cat and a few patches of murky green film referred to warningly by parents as "Ginny Green Teeth". "Keep away from the canal," they would caution their children, "or Ginny Green Teeth will get you!" but, with characteristic disobedience, youngsters armed with small fishing nets and jam jars frequently leaned over the sides, probing into the oozy slime to catch tiddlers. Angling clubs sometimes fed in fish to provide their members with sport, but catches were generally neither impressive nor appetising. Stop-planks were stored at strategic points along the canal banks, and if at any time the ground on either side showed signs of subsidence they were hoisted by crane into the water to prevent flooding and to facilitate rapid repair work being carried out in that particular section. In bad winters the surface froze and people skated on it; barge activity was then halted completely until a thaw set in, when a special boat was sent along first to break up the ice.

During the summer it was customary for a couple of narrow boats to be given a good clean-up and hired out for organised pleasure trips. The horses were bedecked with rosettes, the cargo holds lined with wooden forms and covered with canvas awnings, and liquid refreshment was usually available on board. Evening outings returned fairly late and quite often people living near to the canal were roused from slumber by boisterous and tuneless renderings of "Rule Britannia" and "Clementine" as the barges and their intoxicated passengers sailed by.

Families of canal carriers lived on the narrow boats, tying up overnight at suitable places on the journeys or joining an intimate little community of their own down at the docks, where an ostler would feed and stable the horses for a fee of a shilling a time. Company trustees provided a barge as a floating church for the religious welfare of employees and their families. The men dressed in thick corduroy trousers, collarless flannel shirts, serge jackets, clogs and old seafaring caps frequently worn back to front, and the women in long, voluminous skirts, shawls and high buttoned boots. A few of them (nicknamed "Puffing Pollies" by children) were often seen smoking clay pipes. They all seemed to have a rather peculiar rolling gait and were never seen to hurry.

The boats (named after towns along the canal's route, neighbouring rivers or the wives of company owners) were kept very clean and a collection of gaudily-coloured and well-polished water cans hung from the sides, but the combined living and

*Bridgewater Canal Scene.*

sleeping quarters in the cabin at one end were extremely cramped. Water for domestic purposes was usually hauled from the canal at spots where there were no signs of dead animals or "Ginny Green Teeth". A man, woman or even child steered the rudder, sometimes with a dog or cat curled up lazily beside them, and the family washing was slung to dry on ropes above the cargo. At meal times occupants disappeared into the cabin and always pulled a strip of hessian across the aperture before sitting down to eat.

After they had tied up for a night, adult bargees used to wander into local public houses; the men stayed until closing time and quite often became involved in drunken brawls, but the women took jugs of ale back to the boats for consumption there. They carried outsized baskets when they went to buy necessary foodstuffs from the shops and were noted for scrupulous honesty in such dealings, scorning any form of credit terms - although in view of their constant mobility they would have found it easy enough to evade payment at a later date.

Often several children were housed on a barge but, as they were rarely moored in one place for long, enforcement of regular school attendance was therefore practically impossible. Youngsters from the boats had to register at the nearest school on their first day's stay in a town but seldom attended for more than another couple of days; if it was rumoured that an inspector was checking registers in the vicinity their parents often sent them into hiding until the coast was clear. They were supplied with little notebooks in which the days they spent in school were recorded by one of the teachers, and kept them fastened to a piece of tape hung around their necks - but oftener than not the records were conveniently lost just before they were due for checking.

The kiddies were given special tuition in school but naturally never made much progress, and their rough clothes (sometimes several sizes too large and drawn in around their waists with string) and general timidity didn't help them to mix with the regular pupils. Occasionally it was thought best to isolate them in one special class to suit their infrequent attendances and limited standards. Most of them remained completely illiterate.

Throughout the whole length of the Bridgewater, the barge people were regarded in those days as a little race on its own. Vessels registered for use on the canal reached a peak figure of 1,000 by the end of the 19th century and their trade did not decline significantly until, like all the other waterways in the country, it was affected by the growth of the railways.

Easy canal transportation of materials such as salt from huge Cheshire plain deposits and coal from neighbouring Lancashire mines brought in fresh local industry, particularly the manufacture of soap and chemicals. Resultant thick smoke and acid gas poured into the air and the Mersey was polluted with waste.

The introduction of the tanning industry into Runcorn was at first due to the availability of skins and hides from the county dairy cattle and the oak bark (used in the tanning process) from the 8-mile distant Delamere Forest. During the 18th century, farmers experimented with tanning hides in their own farmyards and, in the next, the trade was established in purpose-built premises. Supplementary materials were afterwards imported from various parts of the world and, with the added bonus of a plentiful supply of essential soft water piped in from Lake Vyrnwy in North Wales, the tanneries prospered substantially and in the course of time became the largest leather producers in Britain.

As termination point of the Bridgewater, the town transformed itself almost unintentionally into a port of some eminence. At the start of the 19th century it had almost 7,000 inhabitants and the docks were filled to capacity with full-rigged schooners which mercenary owners often allowed to be overladen.

My maternal great-grandfather Webster was captain of one of a small fleet of Runcorn-based schooners for a while, and set up home with his wife and two children in a little cottage in a cobbled lane near to the docks, but to earn higher wages he transferred later to a company engaged in carrying slate to Liverpool quays from Port Dinorwic in North Wales. He was drowned during a severe gale in Conwy Bay on 24th January 1871 - after refusing to leave his overladen ship until the rest of the crew had been hauled safely onto another storm-tossed vessel. By the time his turn came the waves were so high and the wind so strong that further rescue attempts had to be abandoned, and three days later his lifeless body was found on the shore near Penmaenmawr. As a tribute to his selflessness on that occasion and acknowledgement of their regard for him as a friendly skipper, his surviving shipmates subscribed a headstone of Welsh slate for his grave (similar to that which had made up the cargo of the ill-fated schooner) and arranged for its inscription as follows:

"Captain Peter Webster (1811-1871)
This stone is the gift of a few friends
as a mark of their esteem of his character."

# CHAPTER 2

The harsh relentlessness of the sea was inflicted upon my ancestors yet again when Peter's son James was drowned off Liverpool on 28th February 1891 at the age of 39. He left behind a 32-year-old widow and nine children - Sara, Emma, Peter and Ann (twins), James, Alice, Miriam, Elizabeth (later my mother) and Jessie (who was then two months old), and an infinitesimal amount of money.

In times of such dire lack of financial support, the newly-bereaved Mrs Webster must have been extremely daunted by the prospect of having to feed and clothe herself and so many youngsters single-handed.

The family lived in a small rented stone house in Mason Street, on the outskirts of Runcorn. It had a tiny parlour from which the front door opened straight onto the street, plus a living room and small kitchen downstairs and three bedrooms upstairs (one with a skylight in lieu of a window). The bedrooms were low-ceilinged and far from large and it is difficult to imagine how my grandparents, two boys and seven girls, could have squeezed into them. There was a long, narrow cobbled yard at the back which contained a wash-house (for both laundry purposes and personal ablutions) and a coal-shed. A gate at the end of the yard gave access to a row of five lavatories on waste ground beyond; all homes in the street were supplied with a key to open identical locks on the doors of each of them, and quite often residents had to wait their turn for one to become vacant. Gaps at the bottom of the doors provided the only light, and slanted wooden slats in the roofs allowed for ventilation (and sometimes the entry of rain drippings!) Users carried along their own toilet paper, torn from old newspapers.

Grandma soon got through her late husband's scant savings and the small sum of "Club" money she gleaned from the Dock Board's Friendly Society after his death and, forced to obtain a regular income somehow, she resolutely converted the little parlour into a shop for the sale of home-made meat pies and cakes, which she baked in the coal-fired oven in the living room. Gas cookers had made their first appearance around 1870 (when gas companies started hiring them out so that people could decide whether they wanted to buy one) but even twenty years later such a facility was still well out of the reach of any of the families in Mason Street. No electrical domestic appliances at all were available to them.

Grandma cooked the meat pies in large flat tins and usually sold them by the slice. The most popular of her cakes were made out of rounds of pastry into which she rolled currants and sugar and brushed with milk to give a burnished effect, but she also did a cheaper variety without currants which were sold as "plain" cakes and buttered on top by the customers themselves.

Unfortunately the shop didn't produce enough cash to meet total household needs, so she decided to take in laundry as well. The only homes able to afford such luxury were situated in a much more salubrious neighbourhood about two miles from Mason Street, and the garments had to be pushed to and fro by one or other of the elder children, on two trucks hammered together from wooden orange boxes and discarded pram wheels. For one shilling a truckful, bedding and clothes were collected, washed, dried and ironed and delivered back to their owners. In summer the young carriers undertook the transportation quite happily but in bad weather they were often forced to take shelter and stand by waiting miserably for a break in the clouds before it could be effected.

Mrs Elwood, who lived just over two miles away in a big house called "The Gables", was one of Grandma's best customers; her husband was the manager of a local soap works and they had a family of three boys and three girls - all of ages convenient for passing on clothes they had outgrown to the Websters. Even shoes and boots which were almost worn out were accepted gratefully and put to further use after being lined with insoles of brown paper, and Grandma used to deposit anything which wouldn't currently fit any of her offspring at the pawn-shop in exchange for a few coppers, and then fail to retrieve them. Mrs Elwood also placed a regular order for pies and cakes (delivered in a basket on top of the laundry) and at Christmas she always sent a bright new penny for each of the children.

Although a shilling was considered quite a goodly sum in those days, the actual laundering process was much more complicated than modern methods. Grandma had first to fill the brick boiler in the wash-house with cold water; for a number of years she pumped it by hand into buckets from a well alongside the lavatories on the waste ground, but later a tap supply of water piped into the town from Lake Vyrnwy was installed in the kitchen of each house in Mason Street. Young Peter prepared the boiler fire from newspaper twists, wood chips and coal slack (sometimes he had to throw on paraffin before it would start up) and refuelling was accomplished by opening the front grating with an iron hook and shovelling on more slack. Once the water was hot, Grandma stirred flaked bar soap into it, immersed the garments (already scrubbed stain-free on a table out in the yard) and slapped a wooden lid on top. After boiling the items for a while she transferred them to dolly tubs full of clear water and helped along the rinsing by hand-swishing a wooden dolly. She also added dolly-blue to the final rinse for garments requiring an extra white finish, and stiffened shirts and loose collars by dipping them into a solution of starch and boiling water.

The clothes were wound manually through a mangle, between two heavy wooden rollers (each about 3 feet long and 8 or 9 inches in diameter) and hung out to dry on a rope line in the backyard with handmade pegs bought from gypsies at the door. A wooden prop lifted the laden line well above the ground and, as Monday was always the main washing day in the neighbourhood, the whole rear aspect of the street was then festooned with garments slapping in the wind like banners. At the end of the wash Grandma emptied the boiler and swilled the yard with cold water - her feet were protected by thick woollen stockings and clogs but her bare hands often became red and swollen in the process.

Sara and Emma had to assist with the ironing, done on top of a calico-covered felt cloth with flat irons heated on the hob in the hearth and rubbed with beeswax for smoother movement; as in most other homes, garments were aired for the following two days on a wooden rack suspended from the ceiling and raised and lowered by means of a rope pulley. In wet weather they had to be dried indoors completely and the room was then clouded by steam rising from the "maidens" on which they were draped in front of the fire.

The whole laundering process was indeed an extremely lengthy and complicated affair, and taking into account the starched shirts, long skirts and innumerable petticoats worn by the gentry at the time, Grandma Webster must have well-deserved her shillings. At least they enabled her to clothe and feed her little brood, although no doubt she would have looked upon the washing machines, biological soap powders and electric irons of later times as manna from heaven.

With ten mouths to fill, the meals she supplied were of necessity simple.

Porridge for breakfast was left to cook slowly overnight in a large pot in the still-warm oven, and during the day broths of barley, carrots, onions and potatoes stood simmering for hours in big iron pans on the hob. Most of the vegetables came from farms at which James and Peter helped out on Saturdays and in the school holidays, and the peelings, dried and wrapped in newspaper, served as additional slow burning fuel for the fire. Meat was bought when the local market was closing down on Saturday night and prices were reduced; most of the remains of the joints roasted for Sunday's dinner were sliced and eaten cold on Mondays, and the rest finished up in stews on Tuesdays.

Favourite meals with the Webster children were "savoury ducks" (made by butchers from fatty scraps of meat and offal), stewed tripe with boiled onions, and small river fluke bought at a penny for as many as a sheet of newspaper would hold from the fishing smacks tied up at a gantry wall along the edge of the River Mersey. Men from similar boats went round from door to door selling shrimps measured in paper cones - twopence picked and a penny unpicked - from large baskets strung from their shoulders on leather straps, and Sunday tea at Mason Street usually consisted of unpicked shrimps (plucked at impatiently by podgy little fingers), and any pies and cakes unsold during the previous week. If, however, the leftover cakes were numerous, Grandma used to crush them with a rolling-pin and blend them together with milk, then bake the resultant soggy mixture between two layers of plain pastry on a flat tin and sell cut into squares as "Wet Nellies" the following week.

On days when household funds were extremely low (for some reason known as "Bally-Ann" days), the children had to be content with thick slices of bread spread with dripping, or were each given a "rouser" to eat (a pancake made from flour and watered milk). As a substitute for a richer egg mix its name could well have derived from the present dictionary interpretation of an "outrageous lie". Fruit was a rare treat - stolen in season from orchards when the boys were delivering the laundry, or bought in doubtful condition from the market late on Saturday night - and sweets were an almost unknown delight.

For a number of years the measure of the family's meagre Christmas fare depended upon the generosity of the local Seamen's Missionary Church, and was mostly limited to a boiling fowl, a plum pudding and a dozen mince pies - all delivered to the house late on Christmas Eve. Christmas presents and festive decorations were never ever in evidence, but Grandma had stored away in mothballs most of the clothes belonging to her late husband (on the assumption that James and Peter would be able to wear them at a future date) and the children used to hang up his long woollen stockings hopefully and usually found an apple, an orange, a few nuts and one of Mrs Elwood's new pennies in each of them the following morning. Their only complaint was that the fruit sometimes tasted rather unpleasantly of mothballs! However, book prizes - in the form of "The Pilgrim's Progress", "Face to Face with Napoleon", "Daisy in the Field", "The Christians" and "Etiquette for Young Men" - were distributed annually at Sunday Schools around Christmas-time, and the young Websters' regular attendances never failed to merit awards.

They went to the Sunday afternoon services at St Luke's Congregational Chapel at one end of Mason Street, the girls (thanks to the generosity of Mrs Elwood) in starched white muslin dresses threaded with coloured ribbons, and the boys clad uncomfortably in handed-down serge suits, high collars and laced-up boots. The collection plate was passed round to the chanting of, "Hear the pennies dropping..." (although in exceptionally lean times buttons were slipped furtively onto it instead) and scholars took turns in going on to the platform to read passages from the Bible. In winter Sunday School officials used to lay on free magic lantern shows during the week, mostly depicting scenes from the Holy Land and to which both children and parents were invited.

By that time there were several churches of varying denominations in the district. The river and canal companies catered considerately for the spiritual welfare of their employees; after a long period of service the barge provided at the Bridgewater docks for that purpose rotted away and was replaced by a Mission Hall, and the Mersey Mission to Seamen also opened a Seamen's Mission in the town. Christ Church, built at Weston Point by trustees of the Weaver Navigation Company, had, due to alteration of river and canal boundaries, become an isolated building on a little island, and five other Anglican establishments included one on the site of the first Parish Church founded by the Mercian Princess Ethelfleda (daughter of King Alfred). Protestant nonconformity spread to Cheshire towards the end of the 18th century and John Wesley preached in the vicinity of Runcorn on a couple of occasions, ringing a handbell to summon people to his open-air gatherings. Growth of Methodism in the area was reflected in the erection of at least seven churches (or chapels, as they were then called). Congregationalism was supported at three local chapels and Presbyterianism at two. Baptists and the Welsh community had their own centres of worship: so did a relatively small number of Roman Catholics.

There was no local hospital until 1903 and there was a constant dread of illness in families because medical attention had to be paid for and even workers who contributed to Sick Societies could ill afford it. Overcrowding and insanitary conditions in homes were responsible for a number of epidemics, and malnutrition lowered resistance to them. In 1905 the 176 cases of infectious disease reported in the town included 30 of scarlet, 43 of enteric and 36 of continued fever, and 48 of diphtheria - and probably quite a few others were undisclosed. The following year there were also some cases of small pox. The fever van (brown, with a distinctive red cross painted on each side) was frequently seen taking affected people to isolation quarters outside Runcorn, and immediately after a patient had been sent off a man from the Public Health Department at the Town Hall went along to fumigate the house. Fortunately there was a noticeable fall in the number of cases of such diseases once the fresh water supply had been piped in from Lake Vyrnwy.

Wearing a shiny top hat, the local doctor used to drive around in a trap drawn by a pony, and often visited patients on his way to and from church on Sundays. Payment for his services was sometimes made in the form of the gift of a few fresh eggs or, in Grandma's case, a large home-made currant cake. On one occasion the doctor noticed young James sitting with his head in his hands on the doorstep in Mason Street and pulled up to enquire into the cause. Told that the lad was suffering with toothache, the doctor took a strand of hair from the pony's mane, threaded it around the molar and with a swift tug ended the agony.

Midwives were familiar figures in the district, dressed in long gaberdine coats and round felt hats and dashing hurriedly with their black portmanteau-type bags to deal with home confinements. Complicated maternity cases were rarely transferred to hospital and young mothers usually died if the midwife or doctor could not cope with difficult births on the spot. Nor was any special care available for premature or sickly babies, and those who were born deformed, or later contracted some long-standing disease, were immediately classed as incurable and pushed around in long cane perambulators for the remainder of their unhappy lives. Club feet, crossed eyes, hare lips, speech impediments and so on were regarded merely as unfortunate and nothing at all was done to alleviate them. Happily none of the young Websters were affected in any such way. For reasons of economy Grandma introduced a variety of home remedies as substitutes for medical treatment. They included goose-grease rubbed onto congested chests and then covered with sheets of brown paper, sulphur blown down inflamed throats, and a mixture of treacle, vinegar, butter and sugar for coughs. She insisted that brimstone-and-treacle was an unfailing cure for persistent adolescent acne, and that styes on the eyes could best be soothed by bathing the affected area with the sufferer's own urine. Her remedy for head colds was "fender ale", to make which she plunged a red-hot poker into a jug of ale and left the brew to keep warm on the fender in front of the fire. The ale could be obtained locally at a penny a pint throughout the day, as public houses were open from early in the morning until eleven o'clock at night. Baby Jessie was the only one of the young Websters who was delicate; all the others were rosy-cheeked and sturdy, although not particularly tall - in fact James and Peter often resorted to the fairly common practice of putting horse manure inside their boots in an attempt to gain height.

The assumption "... if thou criest after knowledge... then shalt thou understand," was certainly not substantiated in the case of the majority of children in Runcorn, who were receiving only minimum tuition in the late 19th century. In all parts of the country education had for a long time been arranged solely by churches and voluntary organisations, and most schools had insufficient places for pupils.

The first school officially opened in Runcorn (in 1811) was the Church of England Parish School, followed by others attached to churches of the same denomination, and three Methodist-based establishments. A Ragged School situated on Mill Brow to cater especially for under-privileged children in its neighbourhood was supported by local subscriptions and the Bridgewater Canal Company made some provisions for kiddies from barges moored at the docks. There were two small Catholic schools.

In compliance with the government's Education Act of 1870, responsibility for elementary education was transferred to locally-elected School Boards, and Board Schools (funded from rates) came into being. Some of the town's existing schools were then re-named and a few new ones were built.

Grandma's youngsters went first to what was originally known locally as the Ragged School at Mill Brow and later to the Boys' and Girls' Board School in Victoria Road, where they were taught reading, writing and simple arithmetic, and current nationwide events were brought regularly to their notice. Written work was carried out on slates, and the girls did needlework and the boys woodwork twice a week. There was no homework. Tuition in extra subjects such as History and Geography could be obtained for a few pence but not many parents (and definitely not Grandma) could afford the necessary fees. The schools were open from 9am to 4pm and there was great delight among scholars when additional holidays were declared for events like the celebration of Queen Victoria's Jubilee in 1897 and the relief of Mafeking in 1900, or when school concerts were organised to support the Boer War Relief Fund.

Attendances of both sexes were frequently poor, chiefly due to epidemics and a general lack of parental interest in education, and sometimes monitors were sent out to look for truants. It was customary for boys to start work between the ages of eleven and thirteen (sometimes even earlier), but girls could not get jobs easily and consequently there were far more girls than boys in the upper classes. Most of them went eventually into domestic service and in readiness for their likely entry into such, my future mother and her sisters were well trained in household chores by Grandma. Children from very poor families suffered frequently from malnutrition and, as their parents could rarely afford the services of a doctor at any time, a medical officer visited schools periodically to check pupils' heights, weights and general physical condition but, as advance warning of his visit was given by teachers (probably to ensure a reasonable degree of cleanliness on the prescribed day), quite a few of the most obviously ill-nourished ones failed to attend for the examination, and its main objective was thus defeated.

No activities were organised for out-of-school hours or holidays. When it was fine girls who lived in Mason Street played out in the street together - at hopscotch, skipping, top-and-whip and trundling hoops - and boys split up for marbles, football and cricket, chalking goalposts and wickets on wooden fences or the sides of houses. Some of them belonged to the Boys' Brigade, whose members marched around to their own band and often brought forth jeers of, "Here comes the Boys' Brigade, all covered in marmalade," from non-participating playmates. There were no facilities for communal indoor recreation, so in wet weather they all tumbled into the nearest wash-house and amused themselves as well as they could. Children of both sexes spent a lot of time filling jam jars with tiddlers from the Bridgewater Canal and often surreptitiously stole the best catches from fishermen's baskets on the towpaths. When the water froze they enjoyed sliding on the ice - at the age of four little Alice narrowly escaped death when she once ventured onto broken pieces immediately after the icebreaker boat had passed by, and had to be hauled back to dry land on the hook of a barge pole. To Grandma's dismay Sara and Emma once brought home a couple of barge waifs with grubby faces and dripping noses, pleading for her to let them join the Mason Street household. She hastily handed over two of her plain cakes wrapped in newspaper and sent the kiddies scurrying back to their canal-based homes.

While Grandma Webster and her little flock struggled to survive in conditions typical of those in poorer class homes in Cheshire just then, the paternal side of my family was enjoying more pretentious surroundings.

My grandfather George Bray was born in 1856 on his parents' farm at Crowland, near to Peterborough. Named after his father, he was an only child and after a happy boyhood left school at the age of twelve to help with the production of the farm's main crops of potatoes and sugar beet. There was no shortage of food in his home and Christmases were celebrated in true Dickensian style with turkey, pigeon pies and all the traditional trimmings, a festive tree surrounded by presents, and carol singers gathering round the blazing hearth to partake of mince pies and ale. Every week young George and his father used to take a load of vegetables by cart to an open market town several miles away, and often returned late at night in a mildly intoxicated state. A girl called Annie was brought to the farm from an orphanage to live in and help in the farmhouse and she and Mrs Bray organised Saturday night hops at which the old man who fiddled the music was also the village undertaker. Well-scrubbed and dressed quite ostentatiously, the family and Annie went to church regularly on Sunday evenings.

Unfortunately, the sudden death of George senior was followed by a domino-slide of cultivation disasters, and when Mrs Bray also died the next year, their son decided to give up the farm. He moved away from his familiar fenland environment of flat fields, ditches and windmills and, at the age of twenty-one, went to work on a smallholding owned by some relatives in Alvanley, not far from Runcorn. Tempted by higher wages, he later took a job in a soap factory in the town and married Martha Hayes, a local girl. They had three sons - Bert (afterwards my father) and his brothers George and Fred - and unhappily Martha died when Fred was born.

Hardship and misfortune seem to have been common denominators in the lives of my ancestors on both sides of the family, although the Brays' circumstances were at least more comfortable than those of the poor Runcorn-based Websters.

# CHAPTER 3

Just over three years before Grandfather Webster was drowned - at the time when the eldest four of his children were attending Victoria Road School, James and Alice were at Mill Brow and the youngest three were still attached to Grandma's apron strings - work had begun on the cutting of a second navigable waterway (the Manchester Ship Canal) through Runcorn.

This was much deeper and wider than the Bridgewater and was built with the intention of providing Lancashire (especially Manchester) and Cheshire with a direct link to the Irish Sea, and thereby make it possible for manufacturers in the area to avoid Liverpool port levies on shipments of raw materials and finished goods, and enter into competition for much-needed expansion of their trade. The waterway was not subject to tides (although entrance to and exit from it were governed by the state of tides in the river estuary) and vessels of up to 12,500 tons could navigate it right through to Manchester at any time. In some stretches it could be used by even larger ships. Its seven-year construction between Manchester and the Wirral involved the employment of a very large labour force and the utilisation of a tremendous amount of mechanical equipment (excavators, cranes, steam pumps, wagons and so on). Runcorn's population increased significantly during all the activity in its neighbourhood and Grandma Webster was disappointed that because of her large family and limited size of home she was unable, like quite a few housewives in Mason Street, to earn extra cash by offering accommodation to incoming workers.

*Manchester Ship Canal and Runcorn Railway Bridge.*

Ocean-going liners passed frequently through Runcorn on the Ship Canal. They towered well above the water but their names, home ports and owners' identifications (Blue Funnel, Ellerman and K lines, etc) could plainly be seen painted on their bows, sterns and funnels, and colourful flags depicted a variety of national origins. Pilots and tugs often accompanied them right out into the open sea in Liverpool Bay.

At Old Quay (near to Mason Street) where a swing-bridge was installed, crews on board ships sailing along the waterway used to sound a hooter to give warning of their approach and a canal employee then quickly closed the gates at each end of the bridge and remained on it as it was swung aside by hydraulic power to allow passage of the vessel. By-standers would wave and shout to sailors on deck, no doubt envying them their journey ahead to more exotic parts of the world; James and Peter were especially thrilled when one day they managed to catch a handful of bananas thrown down by a member of the crew of a Jamaican ship on its way up to Manchester. Now and then liners berthed in lay-byes at the docks at Weston Point so that repair work could be carried out on them, and on one occasion the "City of Poona" was tied up there for a whole month. Oriental sailors on board hired bicycles so that they could get into town easily, and were amazed one day to see the local lads playing football on a patch of waste ground - they had apparently never heard of the game before. Afterwards they formed a team amongst themselves, practised on deck during their stay in dock, and then challenged a bunch of Runcornians to play against them. Unfortunately, it was not discovered until the very last minute that the sailors did not possess football boots and after much argument the teams agreed to play barefooted. The match was drawn but there was no replay!

In some sections of the Ship Canal's route narrow paths ran along the tops of the embankments and, bordered with wild flowers and blackberry bushes in abundance, they provided several miles of pleasant walking space and countless burrow sites for rabbits. After church on Sunday summer evenings there was an almost constant procession of courting couples and parents with young families on the path beside the Old Quay, all dressed in their Sabbath finery. Sadly, Grandma had no time for similar enjoyment and when the children returned from Sunday School she ordered them to sit as quietly as possible at home for the rest of the day. The only game they were allowed to play was dominoes - with a few cardboard pieces cut from an old shoe-box by Ann and inscribed with whatever number combinations she could remember from a friend's authentic set; naturally the games never worked out properly and usually ended in tears of frustration all round.

The development of industry which followed the local siting of the Bridgewater and Manchester Ship Canals necessitated speedy transport across the Mersey estuary of products from factories. The London North Western Railway Company had already erected an iron bridge which carried a double line of rails and a pedestrian footpath over the river and resulted in Runcorn being positioned advantageously on the main line from London to the Midlands and Liverpool, and a Meccano-like Transporter Bridge was also later built between Runcorn and Widnes (the then Lancashire town on the opposite bank of the river) to cater for the passage of motor vehicles and people over the river and Ship Canal. The bridge was bolted into solid rock on either side of the estuary; its 1000ft span was supported on 4 steel towers high above water-mark, and a steel-mesh fenced platform with gates at each end was suspended by steel cables and conveyed across the water. Passengers sat inside a semi-glazed wooden shelter, with motor vehicles (number depending on size) parked alongside. Tolls were collected at little huts and, before the start of each trip, a peak-capped workman used to blow once on a whistle to give warning of departure, then close the separate passenger and vehicle gates, give two further blasts and finally climb a ladder up to the cabin from which his mate controlled the contraption's passage across the water. Crossings were made at 20-minute intervals from either side; if long queues of traffic built up in the approaches to the bridge they were made more frequently, but were always postponed in high winds,. Each one took 5 minutes, although sometimes they had to be halted midway to allow liners with high masts to progress along the Ship Canal, and occasional mechanical breakdowns could result in people and vehicles being suspended over the water for several hours. Children who lived in houses close by often used to dodge mischievously underneath the turnstile at which passengers paid the penny toll, and then hide in the wooden shelter to enjoy a double trip free of charge.

(There was an amusing incident in the bridge's later history, when a member of the Royal Family came to visit the twin towns; the Transporter set off from the Widnes side slightly ahead of scheduled time and had berthed in Runcorn before the welcoming dignitaries were able to reach it from the public house in which they had been sheltering from the icy wind. There was a resultant stampede down to the water's edge, with top hats flying hither and thither, and some of the ladies found it difficult to make appropriate knee-bending curtsies after such unaccustomed exertion!)

The rise and fall of Runcorn's population altered during and after construction of each of the canals, but once the new industries became established it rose steadily. Schools had to be extended, and centres for leisure activity and extra public houses sprang up all over the place. Shopkeepers thrived and found they were able to sell luxury items to a growing number of citizens with improved earnings.

Money was still far from plentiful, though, in overcrowded homes in the many dingy streets. In 1908 a crane driver's weekly wage at the docks amounted to twenty eight shillings and six pence, and widows like Grandma had to struggle on pittance from Friendly Societies and so on until they eventually received official assistance from the government in 1911.

By the end of the first decade of the 20th century it was fairly obvious that trade on the Bridgewater was declining, and the Ship Canal did not prove to be quite as busy as Manchester industrialists had anticipated. But the chemicals works and tanneries had already set the pace for Runcorn's own little industrial revolution, and between 1914 and 1918 made tremendous contributions to wartime demand for their products.

# CHAPTER 4

As the town continued its era of expansion and prosperity, the Webster family slowly disintegrated and in due course left Mason Street.

Jessie died from diphtheria when she was thirteen; Sara, Emma, Alice and Miriam went into domestic service (two of them at a Girls' Boarding school in Southport, where they each received their keep and six shillings a week wages), Ann married in necessary haste, James found employment in one of the chemical factories, and as a ship's boy Peter seemed set to carry on the family's nautical tradition. Elizabeth was kept at home after she left school, to help with the shop and numerous other chores; in those days it was common practice for at least one girl in a family to be assigned to assisting with the general household tasks. All but Peter eventually married and set up their own homes, Sara being the only one to leave Runcorn when she went to live with her husband in Bootle, near to Liverpool.

Just before her 21st birthday, Elizabeth married Bert Bray, and for three years they stayed on in Mason Street with Grandma Webster and Peter. Following a spell of potato-picking on a farm (alongside Irish youths who used to come over to Cheshire annually for the task) Bert went to work at the Highfield Tannery, and when their first child Beth was born he and his wife moved from Mason Street to Highfield Terrace, which was one of several clusters of houses owned by his new employers. A few months after the start of the 1914-1918 War, Grandma abandoned the shop and laundry undertakings and she and Peter joined them there. Bert escaped serving in the war because at the time of the enlistment of his age group he had a severe attack of scarlet fever and was afterwards incapacitated for a long time, and it was not until a few years after the end of the hostilities that he and Elizabeth decided to expand their family.

They were disappointed when I was born as a second daughter, because they had been hoping to name me after Dad's brother Fred who'd been killed in 1915 on active service in France. My brother Fred did in fact materialise two and a half years later, but with lack of foresight in that respect, I was christened (at the suggestion of Aunt Emma who was chosen to be my godmother) with the female derivative Freda.

Highfield Terrace, where I was born, ran parallel with a stretch of the Bridgewater Canal and was built of red Ruabon brick, pebble-dashed on the upper part. The narrow strip of land in front of it was divided into twelve tiny gardens, all edged by a low wall topped with spiked iron railings. Each three houses shared a step and gate leading on to the pavement and occupants were expected to take turns in cleaning the steps. The road alongside was surfaced with small oblong sets, and lorries loaded to absolute capacity with wet hides bounced over them frequently on their way to the tannery, leaving a trail of drippings behind and causing the houses to vibrate to such an extent that deep cracks appeared in the walls. Ours, No. 12, was one of the two end houses which were gabled and slightly larger than the others. It had three bedrooms, a bay-windowed parlour, a living room, kitchen and pantry and a narrow lobby from the bottom of the stairs to the glass-panelled front door. There was no bathroom. A flight of five stone steps went down from the kitchen to a rear yard containing a wash-house, lavatory and coal-shed, and a dirt track separated the yard from a row of gardens beyond. Because of our end position we also had a walled area at the side of the house.

By the mid 1920's our family circle consisted of my parents, my sister Beth, brother Fred and myself, Grandma Webster and Uncle Peter. Grandad Bray and his son George still lived in Runcorn but at some distance from us.

Domestic amenities at No. 12 were limited in many ways. All the cooking was done in the oven in the living room; there was no electricity in the house then and the only gas fitting apart from mantle lights was a single ring in the kitchen. A bath fitted with hot and cold taps and a wooden top with a brass lifting ring lay under the floor in the living room, completely hidden by the hearth rug, but it was considered suitable for the use of adults and Beth only - after the rest of the family had gone to bed. Cleansing of Fred and myself was a major operation undertaken every Friday evening, when a large tin bath was carried up from its hanging place in the wash-house and gradually filled with water; we were washed thoroughly all over with a piece of flannel and carbolic soap. Not for me the Pears' soap whose advertisements at the time pictured a little girl gently massaging her face with their product and thereby "preparing to become a beautiful lady"! As soon as we were dried off we had to kneel in front of Grandma so that she could search our heads for nits with a finely-toothed steel comb. I had no idea what nits looked like nor where they came from, and fortunately none were ever found on us, but I was subjected to specially keen investigation because Mother had noticed that I sometimes played outdoors with a child of dubious cleanliness. After satisfying herself that the probing had been fruitless, Grandma used to wind my hair into tissue paper orange wrappings; although uncomfortable during the night they resulted in flattering curls for a brief period the next morning.

Finally Fred and I were put into clean nightclothes and each given a teaspoonful of Californian Syrup of Figs.

At the age of three I experienced my first taste of calamity just after one of the bathing sessions. The cooking range in the living room consisted of a large coal fire-grate with two round black hobs at the side, and the whole area was surrounded by a heavy brass fender. Our weekday meals fitted in with tannery hours (dinner between 12 and 1 o'clock and tea around 5.30pm) but sometimes Uncle Peter was expected home late from the boat on which he then worked as a stoker, and iron pans were left simmering on the hobs in readiness for his arrival. Trotting across the room that evening I collided with Grandma, who was lifting a pan of broth over to Peter's dish on the table, and some of its piping-hot contents spilled on to my head and neck and scalded me severely. Dad rushed along to the tannery immediately to ask the night-watchman on duty there to telephone for a taxi to take me to the hospital, and I remember quite distinctly that while he was gone, Grandma threw bicarbonate of soda all over my tissue-paper curlers and Mother stripped off my nightdress and put on my clothes once again, even painstakingly fastening the dozen or so tiny buttons on my leather leggings with a button hook. Seemingly oblivious to the commotion, Uncle Peter finished off the remains of the barley broth. I was kept in a high cot at the local Cottage Hospital for several weeks afterwards, and understand that the doctors and nurses there had cause to regard me as an extremely fractious and irritating young patient. Adult inmates, however, fussed around me continually and were quite happy to let me gobble up most of the sweets visitors brought in for them.

At that time meals at No. 12 were planned with economy and Dad's tastes primarily in mind, but at Christmas Grandma was always in charge of the pudding, mincemeat and cake.

Stockings were stuffed with an apple, an orange, nuts and a brand new penny in the toe, and typical presents left at the bottom of the bed were a sewing box for Beth, a book for me and a clockwork train set for Fred. We shared a half-crown selection box of chocolate goodies. Nothing was sent by Aunts and Uncles (nor even by Grandad Bray) but one year Aunt Emma brought the three of us gifts she'd procured by saving up soap packet coupons for twelve months. The same bottles of sherry, port and ginger wine were brought out for several consecutive years. After a big dinner on Christmas Day, we were expected to sit back quietly and enjoy the annual luxury of a coal fire in the parlour. Because it was lit so infrequently, the chimney smoked abominably and the mantelpiece and hearthrug were quickly peppered with soot. Dad, Peter and Grandma nodded off in uncomfortable positions on the rarely-used settee and arm-chairs, and as Mother and Beth appeared on the scene only after they had washed-up a mountain of dishes in the kitchen, Fred and I had ample opportunity to make numerous inroads into the little bowls of sweets, fruit and nuts scattered around the room.

Apart from Christmas presents, the only others we received were those to celebrate birthdays - and they were just small and uninteresting things like pencil-boxes or handkerchiefs - but every Saturday we each got a penny pocket-money. In nearby Halton Road (reached from Highfield Terrace by crossing a narrow iron footbridge over the Bridgewater Canal) there were four sweet shops, and my young friends and I used to spend at least half an hour inspecting the goodies displayed in boxes and jars in their windows before deciding what to buy. Aniseed balls, coconut ice, liquorice root sticks, coltsfoot rock, tiger nuts and cinder toffee were always firm favourites, but we found jelly babies, fairy whispers (tiny sugary wafers conveying messages such as "I love you" and "Kiss me quick"), multicol-

*Saturday - Penny Day.*

oured gob-stoppers and bags of sherbet very tempting also. We never deigned to consider chocolate, because the penny bars were so small, but if ever by some means or other one of us acquired extra cash we used to dash off over the footpath on the Railway Bridge to make an even more specific survey of the confectionery stock at Woolworths in Widnes, where in those days no article was priced above sixpence and you could buy a quarter-pound box of Cadbury's Milk Tray chocolates for that amount. I remember being fascinated by the wrappers on the Fry's sixpenny "5 Boys" chocolate bars there; these pictured a boy's face expressing five different moods (annotated Desperation, Pacification, Expectation, Acclamation and Realization), as his miserable longing eventually culminated in huge enjoyment of the chocolate, but I never felt the bar was big enough to justify my own expenditure.

My pals and I discovered that we could easily obtain coppers from harassed mothers in our neighbourhood by volunteering to push their infants around in prams for an hour or two. We used to meet up in a little group, park the prams en masse well out of sight of the houses and then pass the time playing happily in our own way, turning deaf ears to the babies' howls but carefully scrubbing away their tear stains with a communal grubby handkerchief before taking them back to their respective homes to collect our earnings. My first effort in that sphere of finance miraculously brought in a whole shilling and chanced to coincide with one of Grandma's birthdays. With considerable largesse I spent the full amount on a baker's dozen of oranges for her - I didn't really know whether she liked oranges or not, but I felt I was getting plenty for my money.

In those days of low wages, traders had to compete astutely for custom. There were quite a number of shops in the centre of Runcorn and they stayed open until about 9 o'clock on

Friday and Saturday nights and 6 o'clock on remaining week-days.

Mother bought fish, meat and fruit wherever she was attracted by fresh, reasonably cheap items on display, but she went regularly to the Co-op every Thursday morning for our groceries, and sometimes I went along with her. On Wednesday evening she used to write out a list of her requirements - always beginning with routine necessities such as bacon, sugar and butter - and then make additional entries after a check of stocks in the pantry. At the bottom of the list she showed the amount of bread and coal she wanted delivering to the house during the following week; the bread seemed to arrive without incident, but the men on the coal lorries got customers' orders mixed up constantly, and on those days when they came Fred and I were sent out into the backyard to play, surreptitiously count the number of bags they tipped into the coal-shed, and run back up the steps with the final score before the lorry set off again. We were then ordered to bolt the gate quickly in case the men tried to make use of our lavatory. Mother's weekly fuel order was for two hundredweight sacks of "best" coal, one of "nuts" and one of "slack" (for use on the boiler fire in the wash-house), which allowed for some of it to be shovelled to the back of the shed as emergency stock in case the colliery or delivery men ever went on strike. Any coal dust left in the yard was swept up and sprinkled on the fire in the living room to slow down burning.

We dealt at the Co-op at the town end of Halton Road. The walls on each side of the shop were lined with shelves tightly packed with goods - large japanned canisters of tea and coffee, jars of preserves, tins of fruit and so on, and at the far end there were sacks of sugar, tubs of butter and (protected by a glass screen) hams, sides of bacon and whole cheeses. The floor was sprinkled with dampened sawdust; assistants behind the long, wooden counters were all male, clad in white coats and blue aprons, and the manager also wore a straw boater as a mark of his seniority. In all the years we went to the shop there was no change at all in the staff - they just grew older! Tea, coffee and dried fruits, etc were weighed on large brass scales in accordance with customers' requirements and packed in different coloured bags or cone-shaped twists of thick paper. At exceptionally busy times such as the week before Christmas, some of the goods were pre-packed, but their weights were always checked before they were handed over the counter. Proceedings were delayed somewhat if an assistant had to journey to the back of the shop to slice bacon or cut slabs of butter and cheese and wrap them in greaseproof paper. After prices had been reckoned up and due payment made, customers were given small paper "cheques" in proportion to the amount of money spent, and these had to be taken annually to the Society's office in the town for assessment of individual dividend entitlement. "Divi Day" was quite an event in Runcorn: people used to queue at a local church hall for their appropriate share of the handout and children were kept off school and sent to collect the money if their parents were unable to do so.

The general atmosphere in our Co-op shop was totally different from the mode of later supermarkets. Women stood in little bunches at the counters, waiting to be served and meanwhile getting up-to-date with all the local gossip. Two stools were provided to accommodate infirm customers (who were usually attended to before their proper turn) and I well remember a crafty old lady who regularly used to limp painfully in through the door, receive preferential treatment from one of the stools, and resume her normally active gait once she was outside again. Goods had to be paid for in cash, and if women found after the final reckoning-up that they were short of the full amount, they'd ask for one or two items to be deleted from their orders and make a further visit to the shop after their husbands had received their wages on the following Friday evening.

Every Saturday night Mother took us along to the market in the middle of the town. Fresh fruit and meat, etc, were cheaper than in the shops and there were also numerous stalls (made up with long boards balanced across trestles) selling boiled sweets, books and comics and a variety of other incidentals. A cobbler repaired shoes on the spot, and you were able to get clocks and watches mended at another stall. In the background the Salvation Army livened up proceedings by singing rousing hymns to the accompaniment of their band, and now and then came across to jingle collecting boxes in front of the shoppers. Sometimes a blind man also sat there, begging for alms with an upturned cap, but after noticing how carefully he examined his takings from time to time, I suspected that he was about as blind as the woman at the Co-op was lame.

Quite a few of the stallholders travelled some distance into the market and to Mother's annoyance I habitually crept off to stand and listen to a fascinating man who brought a variety of china, glassware and kitchen utensils from Rochdale.

"Who'll give me five bob for 'em?," he'd call out in a broad Lancashire accent, balancing several plates precariously on two fingers. "No - wait a minute! I've just discovered they're the last of my stock. Not five, four or even three bob! Come on, I know I'm soft in the head, but if anybody'll give me half-a-crown they can have the lot!" At that stage, the surrounding mob of people would surge forward and more and more plates or whatever materialised miraculously - the "last of his stock" never seemed to run dry!

Householders also had plenty of opportunity to buy goods on their own doorsteps. During the week pedlars tramped the streets lugging suitcases bulging with cheap bits and pieces, and offered to sharpen knives and scissors for a few pence.

Apart from in the vicinity of the docks, black skins were almost unique in the district, but most of the pedlars were obviously of Eastern origin and wore brightly-coloured turbans, diamond studs in their noses and large earrings. Gypsies visited the town fairly frequently, laden with baskets full of handmade clothes pegs and eager to give a palm reading in exchange for a silver coin, and signs of long-overdue parental interest in children's education brought forth a flood of encyclopedia salesmen. Men from the fishing smacks moored at the gantry wall still travelled round the streets, although they measured out shrimps in gill and pint cans instead of twists of paper, and sometimes sold cockles as well.

The "Rags-and-Bones" man came into our neighbourhood with his horse and cart every Wednesday. He gave a balloon in exchange for a small bundle of clothing and coppers for larger amounts, and was also usually willing to barter a balloon for a few empty bottles, which he later filled with "Hypo" and sold for use in household drains. In spite of the fact that he'd long since stopped collecting bones on behalf of the local gelatine works, he continued from force of habit to cry out, "Any rags-and-bones, missus?" and whenever I heard him in the distance in my pre-school days I used to scamper swiftly into the house.

"We let him have some old clothes last week," Mother would say crossly, "and the pop bottles aren't empty yet."

"Yes, they are!" I lied repeatedly, dashing down to the wash-house where they were kept and nearly choking myself in an attempt to prove it and get a balloon before the horse and cart passed by.

## CHAPTER 5

As I grew older my next-of-kin at No. 12 became more familiar.

My father was a stockily-built man. He had a very gloomy disposition and was constantly finding fault with somebody or something and writing "I wish to inform you" or "Craving your kind indulgence" letters to the editors of local newspapers and so on to acquaint them with his findings. To him a silver lining just meant that a cloud was close by. He was also prone to long spells of sulking which seemed to be triggered off by quite commonplace occurrences at home or elsewhere (although sometimes the underlying reason might never come to light); without warning his face would take on an expression of extreme annoyance and he then lapsed into a complete silence which inexplicably became more or less communal throughout the whole household. After a few days he would suddenly pass some mundane remark and we could all converse normally once more. Until then meal times, when we sat taciturnly around the table and a nudge and pointed finger had to suffice as a request for the salt or pepper, were especially tedious.

During my schooldays I was sometimes given forms to take home for Dad's signature, and seeing his Christian name shown as Bert, teachers often handed them back, asking for his full name to be shown. "I've told them before - my name is BERT," he would insist, thumping his fist angrily on the table. "But teacher says it can't be!" I pleaded tearfully. "You can't be just Bert - you must be a Hubert or an Albert or something!" In the end, to avoid another sulk or perhaps even a light swish on the backside from the leather strop on which he sharpened his razor, I often squeezed in what I thought was an appropriate prefix to his signature on the form myself. (Only when, at age 70, he was asked to obtain a copy of his missing birth certificate for pension purposes, did he discover that he had been officially registered at birth as Bertram!)

Perhaps his spells of ill-humour were aggravated to some extent by the long hours he spent on a monotonous and messy job at the Highfield Tannery - which at that time was the largest of four in Runcorn. Some of the hides used there were from British cattle, but the majority came from other parts of the world (notably South America and South Africa) and were transported by road from Liverpool docks and made into leather at the tannery for the eventual manufacture of shoes, upholstery, suitcases, saddlery and belting etc in customers' own factories. On arrival at the works the hides were washed and weighed and then sorted to determine the best use to which they could be put; the cheeks, shoulders, bend and belly parts of the skins were individually suitable for making leathers for different types of goods. British ox hides (of unequalled toughness) would be set aside specially for the manufacture of belting to operate machinery from overhead shafts, etc. After de-hairing and treatment in lime and tanning pits, the hides were dried in large sheds, baled in the warehouse and finally despatched in accordance with buyers' orders.

Work in the processing sections was risky at times - men's hands could be caught in the rolling machine, there was always danger of contraction of the dreaded and usually fatal anthrax disease from infected cattle skins and, in 1926, a 16-year-old youth was scalded to death in a vat of hot tannin extract. Dad was employed in one of the tanning pit sheds. His working clothes - thick serge trousers held up by braces, and a short twill jacket with brass buttons (which had to be removed and re-inserted at every weekly wash to avoid crushing in the mangle)

*Highfield Tannery - Drying Sheds.*

smelled strongly of tannin extract, and his fingertips and nails were discoloured permanently by its brown stain. For extra protection when dipping hides into the pits, he tied strips of hessian round his legs.

Most of the men employed at the tannery wore clogs and their clog irons used to clang along the road in front of our house early each weekday morning, followed by the loud blare of a hooter at 7.30 to signal the start of work. Any clanging after that was hurried because it meant that someone was late and in danger of having half an hour's pay stopped. On Saturdays and Sundays there was just a subdued patter on the pavement.

My father was gaffer over half a dozen men engaged on a piecework basis and he had to record the number of hides dipped in tannin and pushed on trucks by each of them to the drying sheds, so that individual wages could be calculated at the end of the week. He completed his reckonings with meticulous accuracy in a little notebook at home and, as children, we were ordered frequently to keep quiet because Dad was "doing his book." The weekly wages earned by a man on piecework in a tanning pit shed averaged about four pounds and ten shillings; and where appropriate, seven shillings were deducted at source for rental of one of the tannery-owned houses. Any necessary overtime contributed a very welcome addition to family funds and, if Dad was asked to turn in for work on a Saturday or Sunday morning, a general air of bonhomie prevailed at No. 12 throughout the weekend. He could have earned more money at the thriving Castner-Kellner chemical works to which some of his mates had transferred, but he always maintained that there was high risk of contamination from toxic fumes there.

Working hours at the tannery were from 7.30 in the morning to 5.30pm, with an hour off for lunch; most of the men lived in the immediate neighbourhood and clocked out for a meal at home. They were also given a 10-minute break at a quarter past ten (known as "bagging time") when they drank lukewarm tea they took into the works each day in enamel cans. A whistle was blown in each of the sheds to mark the beginning and end of the breaks; if workers had overslept in the morning and not had time to make a brew, children were sent along to hand the cans to their fathers at the works' gates at the appropriate time - although management put a stop to that procedure when it developed into a malpractice for merely obtaining the refreshment hot during the winter months. The men queued to receive their wage packets from the pay office on Friday evenings.

In the summer Dad spent some of his leisure time gardening - mainly to ease the family budget. He grew vegetables in the long, narrow back garden and at the bottom of it kept a few hens encased in wire netting. He took great pride in producing colourful clusters of flowers in the small patch at the front of the house and could often be found peering from behind the parlour curtains to make sure that neither of the two sets of neighbours who shared the gate with us had left it open and allowed dogs to stray in and trample his plants. Perhaps because he was slightly deaf and couldn't enjoy musical programmes properly on our battery-run wireless set unless he trumpeted his best ear to within inches of it, he had a passion for the undeniable clarity of brass bands. Each summer one used to perform on fine Sunday evenings in Victoria Park in Widnes (at least two and a half miles from Highfield Terrace) and Mother, Fred and I were forced to suffer his obsession and trudge with him to the park and back on foot. In consequence I loathed the sound of brass bands for evermore. He went to one of the three local cinemas every Saturday night and, sometimes, to watch cricket matches at Lancashire's county ground at Old Trafford, where he claimed to be on very friendly terms with George Duckworth (who at the time was renowned as a wicket keeper). He also belonged to a branch of the Royal Antediluvian Order of Buffaloes (RAOB).

In retrospect it seems sad that Dad had to spend most of his time off work alone - partly because the cost of family outings was prohibitive but chiefly because Mother was so tied down by domestic affairs that she was rarely even able to go to the cinema with him. She was indeed a household drudge. She was quite small, with a faded prettiness, thick black hair knotted into a bun, blue eyes and an up-tilted nose which used to grow so red in winter that I then unkindly dubbed her "Cherry Ripe". Once married, she hardly ever went to church but she always upheld the religious principles instilled by teachers at St Luke's Sunday School and was word-perfect in the hymns she sang as she went about her endless household tasks - her favourites apparently being, "Will your anchor hold in the storms of life?" and "The day Thou gavest Lord, is ended." Perhaps it was literal premise of the latter which caused her to keep fifty rather grubby pound notes in a little cardboard box to ensure, she said, a "proper Christian burial" for herself.

At Highfield Terrace her chores began when she lit the boiler fire in the wash-house in the backyard at 5 o'clock on Monday morning and ended when Sunday supper was cleared away, with a fixed domestic routine throughout the week between. She did all the household cleaning, shopping and most of the cooking. Monday was her regular washday but, in addition, curtains, blankets and bedspreads etc, were laundered during spells of good weather in May or June. Spin-driers were unheard of and Dad had to help her squeeze the heavy, dripping garments through the mangle and lift them on to clothes lines in the backyard and garden. Indoors, pictures and mirrors were taken down and walls and ceilings re-decorated in a massive annual Spring clean. The tannery arranged for their properties to be painted outside periodically (all in the same colour and presumably with a job lot of material obtained at a reduced price) but, to Dad's dismay, tenants were held responsible for interior maintenance. He was far from adept in such requirement and, had he not been an employee at the works, would have undoubtedly been moved to write one of his "Craving your kind indulgence" letters to his landlord on the subject. Despite all upheavals, Mother somehow managed to deal patiently with our childish troubles and ailments.

As my sister Beth was born several years before me, we were never close playmates. She was pale and thin, with two long plaits of straight hair, and always very well-behaved. From a very early age she was troubled by a peculiar nervous disorder which kept her in bed for short spells from time to time. No-one seemed to understand exactly what ailed her but she suffered periodic violent shaking spasms which were probably a mild form of epilepsy and seemed to ease off after a few days' rest. During those she used to amuse herself by making artistic entries in friends' autograph books (a craze just then) or playing patience. Her meals were taken up to the bedroom on a tray, causing me to grumble about such special attention and spitefully nickname her "Blue Eye". Our doctor maintained that the trouble had originated because neither he nor the midwife had been available when Beth was born and that later medical treatment was unlikely to help. For a couple of years Mother took her hopefully every Saturday morning to a homeopathic consultant in Bury; the trips involved a train and two bus journeys and it was often evening before they arrived back home. He prescribed various herbal medicines which had no apparent remedial effect whatever and Dad condemned him disconsolately as, "Just a quack and an expensive one at that!" As Beth got older the attacks became less frequent but to a minor extent, plagued her throughout her life.

I was first aware of the existence of my brother Fred when he took over one end of my perambulator and I watched him slumbering peacefully beneath its big black hood. The pram - a massive affair in which in turn we three young Brays were pushed around - was passed down to us from Aunt Emma and had been used intermittently by most offspring of the original Webster family. It was high and wide, with room for Fred to be pillowed at one end and me (then two and a half years old) to perch on a detachable seat at the other. On shopping days I was left in Grandma's care so that Mother could pile her purchases underneath and on top of the seat.

As a child Fred was plump and extremely docile. I got on well with him, perhaps chiefly because he allowed me to have the upper hand in all our childish pursuits without question. I remember continually repeating a little rhyme to him:

"Adam and Eve and Pinch-me-tight
Went down to the river to bathe;
Adam and Eve were drowned
So who do you think was saved?"

Of course, he said, "Pinch-me-tight" and I did - quite fiercely. After the first time he was fully aware of what would follow but obligingly always made the requisite reply. If we played hide-and-seek, I was always the one to hide and he to seek. If ever we found a dead bird, I made him dig a hole for its burial and stand by holding it patiently while, with tears streaming down my cheeks, I said a little prayer committing the smelly remains to the arms of Jesus. He made rather slow progress at school and was often used as a scapegoat for the gang of boys in our neighbourhood. If eggs were found smashed in hen coops, gardens raided or rubbish set alight, Fred was always blamed, but he just denied the accusations placidly and never named the real culprits.

It was Grandma Webster, however, who really dominated the family circle at No. 12. Photographs of Queen Victoria show that she and Grandma resembled each other quite closely in both features and stature. They also each produced nine children! Grandma had a short, straight nose, piercing blue eyes and hair parted in the middle and drawn severely into a tight bun at the back of her head. About five feet tall, her apparent frailty was deceptive, because her determination and capacity for endurance were as inflexible as her tiny tightly-corsetted form. She was born in Liverpool and came to Runcorn as a bride in her early teens; before that she had earned her keep and a few shillings a week as parlour maid at the home of a prosperous wine merchant on the outskirts of the city. Apart from the gingham aprons she wore around the house she always dressed completely in black. At that time most widows wore black habitually for the first twelve months of the mourning period and then progressed through black and white to purple and grey. Grandma, however, never relinquished her total sombre black - again a fashion adopted by Queen Victoria herself.

Grandma organised our domestic affairs and settled all disputes beyond argument from her rocking-chair alongside the fireplace. She did no housework whatever but always kept a firm control on any cake and pie-making; no-one else was permitted to even assist with that. Grit and resilience had carried her through difficult days in Mason Street (in fact at times she must have survived by sheer determination only) but at Highfield Terrace she apparently aimed at enjoying creature comforts to the full.

A jug of hot water and a cup of tea had to be taken up to her bedroom at 9 o'clock each morning and she didn't come downstairs until she reckoned that the newly-lit fire would have warmed up the living room. Her breakfast always consisted of several rashers of smoked bacon with fried bread, followed by well-buttered toast and a pot of coffee. Every night she sipped a tablespoonful of whisky in hot water and a warm oven shelf or brick, wrapped in a piece of flannel, was put into her bed an hour before she retired. She also dosed herself frequently with Castellan Cough Mixture, so named after its place of manufacture in Castle Street in Liverpool, not because she was prone to coughs but because, she said, it helped her to sleep soundly. She obviously intended, by all available means, to maintain her excellent health. Due to limited accommodation, Beth and I were compelled to share a second bed in the room in which she slept. Unfortunately I was allocated a place immediately under the gas light fixture and had the task of standing on tiptoe on my pillow each night to turn out the mantle light as soon as we were all in bed. Grandma's undressing involved the removal of several layers of petticoats, drawers and stays. To me this was seemingly endless and, with drooping eyelids, I often used to entreat her impatiently to get a move on. My chidings invariably brought forth the lament, "I can see I'm not wanted here, Lord - so please take me to heaven in my sleep tonight," and once, overcome by tiredness, I muttered under cover of the bedclothes, "I wish He would!"

Members of her family, who'd settled elsewhere with their various spouses, came to visit her spasmodically at Highfield Terrace. She took a keen interest in their doings and didn't hesitate to level strong criticism in their direction whenever she felt it was justified - which appeared to be very often. A few days before her 70th birthday she announced that, as she was "not long for this world," she was inviting them all to a tea-party at No. 12. The event was in fact repeated on 8th June every year afterwards until she died at the age of 87! Mother, of course, was encumbered with most of the necessary preparations.

Grandma was a staunch Methodist. On Sundays she went to morning service at St Paul's Wesleyan Methodist Church and on Tuesday evenings to the Ladies' Class there. For those occasions she dressed in a long black skirt and bodice, a silk cape with a ruffle round the neck, a black hat held in place by beaded hatpins, calf-length boots and lace gloves. She carried a large black umbrella (whatever the weather) and her own hymn book, and used to turn through the massive wrought-iron gates at the front of the building like a pint-sized Ship Canal liner drifting into the docks. On Tuesday evening the coincidental clanging of bells from the ringers' practice session at All Saints' Parish Church provided a fitting accompaniment to her regal entry. She once took me to one of the meetings and, when the visiting Negro spiritualist invited all the ladies to join in with the chorus of a song, I watched fascinated as she stamped her feet and the umbrella, chanting vehemently:

"Climb up, ye little children,
Climb up, ye older people -
Climb up to the skies!
Now is the time for heaven,
Climb up in six and seven,
Climb up, ye people, climb!"

Although she showed little sentiment towards anyone, Uncle Peter was definitely the apple of Grandma's eye (perhaps because he was her only unmarried surviving offspring) and she looked after him like a mother hen with a chick. He was small and wiry, with the twinkling blue eyes possessed by all of the Websters, closely cropped hair and a rather large nose. In due course he progressed from ship's boy and stoker to first

47

mate on boats owned by William and Henry Cooper of West Bank dock at Widnes, which were engaged mainly in dredging sand and gravel from the Mersey and carrying it into Liverpool. Until proper river-dredging equipment was fitted to the boats the crew shovelled sand cargoes manually into the holds from sandbanks near to Ellesmere Port. Peter worked very long hours - in wartime (when his job exempted him from Forces service) often for over twenty hours at a stretch - and whenever his boat docked after the Transporter's last nightly trip at 11pm he faced a long walk home via the iron bridge over the river. His comings and goings were governed by the tides and there was always the possibility of his reaching No. 12 at any time of day or night. Although he showed up only occasionally during the week, he was usually at home for part of the weekend and, on Sunday nights, Grandma used to make up a basketful of provisions (ready-baked meat pies, currant cakes, egg custards, tinned condensed milk and so on) for his consumption on the boat in the days ahead.

Uncle Peter was a keen disciplinarian and, in spite of smoking twenty full-strength Capstan cigarettes every day, professed to aim at keeping his physical fitness strictly up to the mark. Each morning he exercised for about ten minutes, flinging his arms upwards and outwards and pronouncing aloud:

> "Now is the time for me to rise
> And shake the slumber from my eyes;
> To hail the East and greet the West
> And say to God: I'll do my best."

He quite often expressed an interest in politics - although he had no real knowledge in that field and, in fact, from time to time transferred his support to whichever party seemed to be catering currently for his own personal benefit. The most outstanding trait in Peter's character, though, was his excessive miserliness. He paid twenty-five shillings a week direct to Grandma for his keep but never contributed to any general household amenities and, by helping himself repeatedly to our domestic stock of shoe polish, matches and so on , undoubtedly gave rise to quite a few of Dad's sulks. He earned high wages and accumulated a considerable number of gold sovereigns and silver pieces which he hoarded in old shoe boxes in his bedroom and totted up every Sunday morning. He also deposited money regularly in a couple of banks. One year the interest paid by the Co-op bank was so low that he decided to withdraw his investment at once. The staff there tried to dissuade him but he remained adamant and, in the end, the manager spitefully handed over the total withdrawal in loose silver, which Uncle Peter (dressed in his best suit) and I carried home in two shopping bags.

The hoarding seemed to become an obsession with him. At one time my parents tried to persuade him to help them buy a newly-built house (with four bedrooms and a bathroom) at a cost of £495. They were proposing to use Mother's £50 burial reserve as a deposit and borrow the rest from Peter on a weekly repayment basis, but he flatly refused to co-operate. He was, however, always willing to assist with any economies. In those days coal was taken to the Highfield Tannery on Bridgewater Canal barges and hauled into the storage shed by means of crane and skip. As the skip swung away from the boat and above the towpath small bits of coal were shaken out of it and, whenever Peter saw a vessel heading for the works, he used to hurry along with a bucket to collect the droppings for future use on the boiler fire in the wash-house. He also shovelled horse manure from the towpaths for fertilising Dad's potatoes. Those and other self-imposed tasks were often undertaken in rain or even snow.

All I remember of Grandfather Bray is that he had a deep, throaty chuckle and on his rare visits to Highfield Terrace he used to pat me on the head and, after I'd recited the Lord's Prayer to his satisfaction, invite me to dip into a large bag of extra-strong peppermints which he always seemed to carry in his pocket.

He was a dapper man of short stature, with a rather prominent Roman nose and a neatly-trimmed moustache. He took great pride in his appearance and, in his pinstripe suits, immaculate high starched collars and well-polished boots, was reputed to be one of the best-dressed men in the neighbourhood. After working in the soap factory for several years, Grandad 'bought' an insurance book and went round from door to door collecting premiums. In those days people earning low wages tended to have large families and, of course, dreaded the possibility of having to pay burial fees. Most children's lives were insured immediately at birth because the infant mortality rate was so high. In 1905 the deaths of 66 babies under one year were recorded in Runcorn and a gravestone in the cemetery there confirming that three children in one family died at the ages of two, five and nineteen months respectively, is by no means unique. Grandad was liable to be called out at any hour by parents wishing to open a policy on the life of their newly-born baby and, if they weren't able to keep up the necessary payments later (usually a penny a month for each child), he sometimes subscribed them temporarily out of his own pocket rather than lose custom by closure of the policies.

Naturally, I have no recollection whatever of Grandma Bray, who had died many years before I was born, but in a silver-framed sepia wedding photograph in the parlour at No. 12 she was pictured perched on a high stool beside her young husband, looking very solemn and wearing a dark silk dress with tiny pleats all the way across her ample bosom, and a large hat trimmed with artificial flowers and berries. He appeared equally grave in a double-breasted tweed jacket with a velvet collar and a little cap. The background of the picture showed Highland cattle grazing below mountains whose tops were hidden in swirls of thick mist and gave the impression that the couple must have pledged their troth somewhere in the wilds of Scotland, but apparently the scene had been added merely to produce an artistic finish, in accordance with the practice of professional photographers just then.

Grandad Bray went into lodgings when his son George moved away from Runcorn, and seemed to have a very lonely existence afterwards. To me they both faded quickly into obscurity but Mother and Dad, Beth and Fred and Grandma and Uncle Peter featured significantly throughout my childhood.

# CHAPTER 6

When I was young the admittance of children into Runcorn schools was rather haphazard and, although five was considered to be the most suitable age for first attendance, enrolment at times depended to some extent on the size of the classes already in existence. I began my education at Mill Brow School at the age of four and a half. Its former title of Ragged School had by then been abandoned and, after being utilised as a Board School until it could no longer cope with the increasing intake, it had become an infants' department for the nearby Victoria Road Boys' and Girls' School.

Mill Brow was built in dark brick with one gabled end and to me (under three feet tall) from the inside the sky only was visible through the high, narrow windows. It had two large classrooms, a wide entrance hall which also served as a cloakroom, a yard surrounded by a high wall, and an outside lavatory. As teachers disappeared completely from time to time I suppose there must have been a staff room somewhere, but I never saw it.

The fact that the lavatory was in the singular reminds me instantly of an incident in my very early days at the school. A little girl who had been in my class and whose home was close by had died. At her parents' request, pupils were lined up and sent to walk around her coffin in their parlour. Most of us quaked at the invitation but, on a quick peek through half shut eyes, were quite relieved to see her apparently sleeping peacefully, holding a white lily in each hand and looking just like a wax doll. The bunch of flowers towards which we had each contributed a ha'penny lay at her feet. Her mother stood on the front step, admitting us in small groups and, as we shuffled through the open door, declared tearfully that Olive had died because she had had to queue so long to use the lavatory in the playground. I think one of the teachers must have heard about the accusation, however, because the crocodile was halted abruptly just before the second class joined in.

Infants' teachers were then generally female and not usually married. The head teacher at Mill Brow taught the senior class; while I was there she was an enormously stout lady with untidy hair who wore rimless spectacles on the end of her nose. Her desk was alongside the furnace which heated the building and pupils who gave a good account of themselves were given the dubious honour of re-stoking the fire. Another reward for diligence was to be sent by her into the town on errands and my mother was disagreeably surprised one afternoon to find me, at the age of six, standing proudly in a very long queue at the main Post Office.

The teacher of the beginners' class was much younger than the headmistress but equally stout. She rang the bell at the beginning and at the end of lessons and playtimes and also thumped out a brisk tune on the piano in a corner of the hall as we lined up in the yard and then marched into the classrooms. She was continually muttering to herself, "See a pin and pick it up and all day long you'll have good luck," and bending down with great effort to retrieve pins from nowhere to stick onto her chest, with the result that at times she looked like a plump pin cushion. Each Friday she gave a few sweets to the child in her class who had been best-behaved that week. Boys were punished for bad behaviour by three strokes of a cane across the backside from the headmistress and anyone who chattered too much got their mouth sealed with a piece of sticking plaster and was made to stand in a corner for one hour. Dull-witted pupils were given large paper caps to wear, which had "Dunce" scrawled across the front of them. Assortments of barge children joined the beginners' class spasmodically and often disappeared overnight.

We had lessons in reading, writing and arithmetic. Reading was accomplished by phonetic recognition of the letters of the alphabet and the walls of the beginners' classroom were covered with pictures depicting 'a for apple', 'b for ball' and so on. We must have found it difficult to appreciate that letters like c and k could sound alike or otherwise in different words, yet the majority of pupils seemed to master it easily enough. Writing was done with pencils with rubbers at the end and arithmetic consisted of simple additions and subtractions and reciting multiplication tables from charts hung over the blackboard. There were no sandpit or "play-way" teaching methods of any kind at Mill Brow, although in the beginners' class we had to lean forward on our desks with heads on arms for ten minutes every afternoon. In the first year infants were seated in order of surname, but in the second streamed into groups according to standards of intelligence. I was a quick learner and was placed at one of the shared desks in the front row of the top group, but most of my little friends were at the back of the room and seemed to have a far more enjoyable time because they were not so close to the headmistress's eagle eye.

After two years at Mill Brow I moved on to what was by then Victoria Road County Primary School, where boys and girls were segregated into two separate parts of the building, each with its own entrance and playground. Girls occupied all the upstairs classrooms and the boys the ones at ground level.

Our education was expanded to include English, History, Geography, Scripture and Needlework (or woodwork for the boys). Each teacher, except the head, taught all subjects to one class for one year. Scholars were provided with individual desks and wrote with pens and ink (two monitors were elected weekly to wash and refill the inkwells). On Monday mornings the first half-hour was set aside for the collection of school bank and milk money and you could buy a dozen Horlicks tablets for three pence to make the milk more palatable.

Examinations were held at the end of every school year, with book prizes for those who got the highest total marks in each class. I managed to win two prizes during my four years at the school but was always handicapped by the low marks I was given for needlework, which I detested. For that we had to supply money for the cost of material for a pinafore or some such simple garment cut out by the teacher and hem and embroider it ourselves. I'm afraid my hemming stitches usually resembled dogs' teeth, and stems of my embroidered flowers became entwined in all the wrong places. Everybody else had completed whole sprays of wild roses and violets before I'd even shakily sketched in the rough outlines. At one stage the sewing was replaced by raffia-work and I prayed that my clumsy fingers might somehow manage to twist the lengths of coloured fibre into table mats etc with the same skill as the others, but I fared no better. At the end of one of the lessons the teacher discovered that several skeins of raffia had disappeared and kept us all behind to identify the thief. When no confession was forthcoming we were all forced to empty our pockets and then as a last resort to turn down our knickers; the raffia fell from the pants of the girl Mother had deemed to be likely to pass on nits to me.

Most pupils went home for lunch except on Fridays, when there was a midday break of half an hour only (in which we ate sandwiches at our desks) and the school closed half an hour earlier. The afternoon was then devoted to games in the playground; classes split up into teams and wore red, green or yellow braid sashes to show which one they represented. The

*Victoria Road School, Runcorn.*

games consisted mainly of relay and leapfrog races and round-ers. In wet weather we practised country dancing indoors; perhaps it used to rain fairly frequently, because in 1929 a team of dancers from Victoria Road won first prize at the Liverpool Festival.

The school was opened to parents for half a day each year to enable them to see samples of our best work (pinned to the walls in the various classrooms) and to chat with the teachers. There were no organised Sports Days nor official prize-givings but we were occasionally offered cheap tickets for special Saturday morning matinees at local cinemas, when films of some educational significance were being shown - for example, "Trader Horn" which was reckoned to familiarise us with Africa. At Christmas pupils with dramatic, singing or dancing ability were chosen to perform at a concert in front of the rest of the school.

Doctors and dentists from the County Health Depart-ment travelled around Cheshire visiting schools and they came to Victoria Road once a year. If medical attention was consid-ered justified after an examination, you were given a sealed note to take home to your parents and for dental treatment were sent to a local clinic, where for a fee of sixpence any necessary number of teeth were extracted (never filled) - with-out an anaesthetic of any kind. The most common medical advice was a recommendation for minor operations on tonsils and adenoids; when it was decided I needed such treatment Mother walked me to the Cottage Hospital one morning and came to collect me by taxi in the afternoon. One of the nurses made me feel superior to the other temporary patients by recollecting my previous stay there after the scalding, but I was disappointed that I wasn't kept in overnight on this occasion as I'd hoped to impress classmates with an exaggerated account of the operation.

The closest friends of my early schooldays were Joyce Hankey, Dorothy Dawson and Maureen Crampton.

My friendship with Joyce was tragically short. She and her younger sister were orphans who came to live with their widowed grandmother in Highfield Terrace after their mother had died of tuberculosis (then known as consumption). They were rarely allowed outside the house but I was often invited to play card and domino games with them and the old lady tried in vain to teach me how to knit and do crochet-work. The girls' father had been a Freemason and fellow members offered to pay for them to be educated at a boarding-school as soon as they reached a suitable age. Unfortunately a school medical examination revealed that Joyce, too, was consumptive and she was sent for treatment in a sanatorium on the edge of Delamere Forest. We wrote several little letters to each other and after a few months our teacher took me to see her. On a bitterly cold day I was appalled to find her lying in a high iron bed out on an open balcony. She coughed continually and her cheeks were bright red; after hearing a nurse whisper to the teacher that her purple toes could be a sign of approaching death, I quickly handed her the book I had taken and retreated into the draughty corridor. I coughed incessantly all the way home in an attempt to rid myself of the TB germs I felt certain I'd picked up. Poor Joyce did die very soon afterwards and her grandmother insisted that I should go to the funeral, walking with her up the cemetery path behind the little coffin on which I put a bunch of daffodils from our garden.

I must have been almost seven years old when Dorothy Dawson came perceptibly into my young life. In many ways she was to be more of a rival than a friend. She was an only child, very pretty, with china blue eyes and long fair hair which hung down to her waist in ringlets and was tied back with satin ribbons. From my "top-stream" position at the front of the class at Victoria Road School I often eyed her (seated several rows behind) with admiration and envy.

I was overjoyed when one Saturday morning Dorothy and her parents moved into a house in Churchfield Terrace, also owned by the Highfield Tannery, in what I thought was grand style - although Grandma prophesied darkly, "Saturday flit, short sit." Mr. Dawson was employed in the firm's warehouse and had working connections with the Bridgewater Canal Company. Their belongings were transported to their new abode on an open cart pulled by a canal horse, with Dorothy seated regally on top of a table. I trotted alongside for the last few dozen yards, thinking that in her frilly dress she looked just like a princess on a throne. The houses in Churchfield Terrace were superior to ours and had bathrooms. Once the Dawsons had settled down, Dorothy's mother encouraged her to take playmates home and, for some inexplicable reason, this often included an invitation to watch Dorothy take a bath. Whenever I was lucky enough to be chosen I used to perch on a cork-topped stool in a corner of the bathroom and gaze enviously at her lashings of hot water, duck-shaped soap and soft pink towels. After she'd been dried off, her mother tucked her into a fluffy dressing-gown appliqued with little lambs and wound her long hair into ringlets with strips of calico - much more efficient than Grandma's tissue paper wrappings. I think those bath-times instilled into me my first awareness of class distinction!

When I first became friendly with Dorothy she possessed piles of indoor games, a twins' pram with a rosy-cheeked doll at one end and a little piccaninny at the other, a rocking horse, a fairy cycle and also a Great Dane, two Angora rabbits and a parrot. Beside her many toys my skipping rope and a yo-yo seemed painfully insignificant, and we'd had pets at No. 12 for two brief periods only. One was a mongrel which disappeared mysteriously after Grandma had tripped over him twice and the other a tortoise I persuaded Mother into buying for me at the market one Saturday night - when I got home I found I was terrified by the small beady eyes peering out above its scraggy neck, and was quite relieved when it died a week later!

Dorothy and I walked to school together and on weekday mornings I used to call for her much earlier than necessary in the hope that her mother would give me a few of the sweets she stuffed into her daughter's pockets. In the shortened Friday lunch breaks most pupils munched meat paste or hard-boiled egg sandwiches, but Mrs. Dawson used to arrive at 12 o'clock sharp with a basket containing hot pies, cutlery and even a napkin for my friend. There was no stipulated uniform at Victoria Road and girls usually wore economically plain navy or grey skirts and blouses or jumpers. Dorothy, however, came along in crocheted dresses in a variety of pastel shades, with frilly petticoats underneath and matching ribbons in her hair. In the winter she had pleated plaid skirts and Fair Isle sweaters and kept her hands warm out-of-doors in a white fur muff. Pretty and pampered, she did indeed seem to possess all the attributes and advantages needed to ensure a comfortable passage through life.

My friend Maureen Crampton was nearly twelve months older than me and something of a tomboy, with straight hair, an infectious giggle and a piercingly loud voice. She was the only girl with whom boys in our neighbourhood would play marbles and she acquired a good collection of "glass allies" at their expense. She had an older sister from whom she used to borrow most unsuitable clothes and steal nail varnish to paint on to her own dirty finger nails.

That friend led me astray in many ways - one by introducing me to the art of petty stealing when we went to spend our Saturday pennies. One of the shopkeepers in Halton Road kept jars of sweets stacked on shelves right up the ceiling and used a stepladder to bring down those near the top. Maureen would ask purposely for something he couldn't reach easily and, as soon as his back was turned and he'd begun to climb the ladder, fill her pockets with goodies from the counter. In winter her parents and older sister went to the cinema every Saturday night and the two of us had the run of their house. We then plastered our faces with her mother's make-up, heated curling tongs in the fire and frizzed-up our hair, baked potatoes in the oven, and generally had great fun - even by Maureen's standards. Sometimes she searched for spare coppers in the drawers or the pockets of her father's best suit and, if she was successful, we tripped along to the chip shop in Halton Road to buy bags of "mixed" (chips and mushy peas). We also went round pressing button Bs in telephone kiosks periodically in the hope of gleaning a shoal of coins. Around Christmas time we swelled our finances by carol singing, although we never gave much value for money before we banged on the doors and chanted:

"Knock on the knocker, ring on the bell-
Please put a penny in the old man's hat;
If you haven't got a penny, a ha'penny will do,
If you haven't got a ha'penny, God bless you!"

Happy Days! By that time I think effects of the country-wide depression must have taken their toll in Runcorn, but I only remember that the lorries bounced along the road to the tannery less often, Dad sulked over his lack of overtime and I got a bit more for my Saturday penny because prices in the shops were reduced.

# CHAPTER 7

Long before home television and family holidays abroad were in vogue, I had no difficulty whatever in getting plenty of enjoyment from a variety of simple activities in Runcorn.

One was an annual Children's Treat arranged by the Co-operative Wholesale Society, for which tickets were distributed to customers in proportion to the amount of money they'd spent at the society's shops in the preceding year. Children participating were told to assemble at a given time in front of the Puritan Tannery in Halton Road and trailed circuitously on foot through the town to a plantation about two miles away. Coal lorries and milk floats advertising Co-op goods chugged slowly at the head of the procession and annoying delays occurred if one of them broke down. When we arrived at the plantation we had to form a queue along one side of the field and were each given a paper bag containing an apple or an orange, a wrapped chocolate biscuit, and a few boiled sweets made at the CWS factory in Crumpsall. There was no entertainment of any sort so we just messed around amongst the trees for a while and then wandered wearily home. Fred attended that event once only.

Another Treat, organised every year by the Royal Antediluvian Order of Buffaloes for members' children, was a much grander affair, with a knife-and-fork tea, a small present for everyone and a fancy dress competition. One year Mother borrowed a Dutch boy costume for Fred to wear, but the clogs with it didn't fit him; after hearing that someone had seen a pair which appeared to be a suitable size hanging on the wall inside a local pub, she sent Dad off to ask whether the landlord would be willing to loan them out. No-one was exactly sure where the clogs had been sighted and after visiting The Grapes Inn, The Navigation, The Devonshire and The Traveller's Rest without success (and feeling obliged to buy a pint of beer at each of them) he reeled into The Glass Barrel, where his slurred request for a pair of Dutch clogs was treated with infinite suspicion all round and he was advised to make his way home without further delay! I once entered the competition as a Balloon Girl, with the strings of several coloured balloons pinned to my best dress and won the consolation prize of an HMV gramophone record, with "O for the wings of a dove " on one side and "The Laughing Policeman" on the other. Unfortunately we didn't possess a gramophone at No. 12 at the time.

May Day celebrations in our district took the form of small processions of youngsters around the various streets and were organised mostly by themselves. Girls from Highfield and Churchfield Terraces combined forces for the event and we used to wander round the neighbourhood in a little group headed by a May Queen dressed in her Sunday frock and carrying a bunch of flowers (often plucked without permission from someone's garden) and the rest of us with crepe paper streamers dangling from circlets round our heads. The main object of the exercise was to extract "a penny for the May Queen" from householders and our takings were spent on iced buns which we ate in the backyard of the current May Queen's home. One year we heard that a shop at the far end of the town had the previous day's unsold cream buns on offer at a third of the normal price and, thinking that our little gang would be in for a special treat, Maureen and I dashed off as soon as we'd collected enough coppers to get two for each of us. We were all violently sick shortly afterwards.

A different Queen was usually chosen by ballot each year but we were so impressed by the marvellous spread laid on for us at Dorothy's when it was her turn (we were even invited to sit down at the table in the kitchen) that we voted unanimously that she should take the regal role on all future occasions.

One of the most popular happenings in Runcorn took place in July, when a big carnival was held for the benefit of local charities. The carnival procession was routed through most of the town and included brass, silver and jazz bands in colourful costumes, troupes of dancers and decorated tableaux on foot, carts or lorries. Before they set off, the various tableaux and individual fancy dress entrants were judged by a committee and successful ones exhibited cards indicating the class of their award. Spectators stood along the pavements and threw money onto the passing vehicles and progress was halted from time to time while the dancers performed in the streets to glean extra cash. The focal attraction in the procession was the Carnival Queen, seated on the largest lorry and surrounded by a retinue of attendants. She wore a long white satin dress embroidered with imitation pearls and a purple velvet cape edged with mock ermine. At her feet a pageboy in velvet knickerbockers and satin blouse held a cushion bearing the magnificent diamante headpiece with which she was to be "crowned". The procession wound slowly through the streets to the football field where, amidst much clapping and band playing, the Queen was crowned. After gymnastic and dancing displays the event culminated in a confetti battle at dusk.

The dress and paraphernalia of the Queen and her retinue were always put on show in one of the local shop windows well before the day and I used to eye them longingly and hopefully practised sedate steps and regal bows in the backyard at home (with an old net curtain hanging from my head and wielding the yard brush as a sceptre) in case the majestic honour should ever come my way. The Queen and her attendants were chosen by drawing from the names of all Runcorn

Sunday School scholars of requisite age; alas, my name never came out, although I was surprised and very gratified that Dorothy's didn't either.

Only once did Maureen and I manage to take an active part in the proceedings - after it was decided one year that the Queen crowning ceremony should be replaced by a visual narration of the story of King Alfred's daughter, Ethelfleda, the Mercian princess who had built the first castle and parish church in the district. Ethelfleda and her entourage were chosen in the usual way but an additional hundred juvenile volunteers were sought to make up a tableau representing waves in the River Mersey. Maureen and I responded with such alacrity that we were put in the front row and in dresses of blue and green net we held hands and swayed rhythmically to music as we set the pace for the remainder of the waves accompanying the lorry bearing Ethelfleda and her boat across the football field. It proved to be rather exhausting.

A November Wakes holiday had been celebrated in Runcorn every year since 1889 and activities included a fair set up on waste ground on the outskirts of the town. I used to prowl around the site long before it was opened officially, fascinated by the burly fairhands and their caravans with well-polished brassware and jugs of artificial flowers. One of my school prizes had been a book called "A Peep Behind the Scenes", the story of a young girl who ran away from home to live with gypsies and, dazzled by the apparent glamour of her nomadic existence, I told Maureen that I was thinking of doing likewise.

"These here aren't real gypsies," she declared scornfully in her penetrating voice. "They're just fakes - proper Romanies live in tents and don't have bobby-horses and coconut shies and what not!"

"What about the one with a red spotted handkerchief round her head who sits behind that curtain and tells fortunes?"

"Bet even she's not a real one, either - only daubs her face to make you think she is!" was my friend's phlegmatic reply. "Probably uses Miner's liquid make-up - Dark Ochre, I bet, like my Mam got at Woolworths in mistake for Blush Pink. Made her look like a Paki, my Dad said. And they keep the booth dim inside, so you can't see anything properly. Mind you," she added grudgingly, "if it's the one who came last year, my Aunt Elsie reckons she really knows her stuff. She told her there was a dark, handsome man waiting to marry her and take her round the world."

"Gosh! Where's your Aunt Elsie now?" I queried, open mouthed.

"Still working at Glover's Laundry in town. The only dark man there is the boss and he's married already and got three kids. Maybe the right chap hasn't shown up yet," Elsie's young niece hazarded hopefully.

At night the fair was lit all over with twinkling lights and the strains of "A life on the ocean waves" and "Good night, ladies" blared out monotonously from an electric organ until midnight. There were bobby-horses, dodgems, and a wall-of-death and chair-planes, but my favourite form of entertainment was a three-minute spell in the huge swingboat with a canvas top in which you were gradually swept upwards into an almost vertical position. People queued to see the Fattest Woman on Earth, the Man with Five Chins, and the Amazing Midgets and to buy swirls of candy floss, or perhaps doughnuts dipped into a pan of sizzling oil on the spot. At amusement stalls you could roll pennies on to numbered squares (if successful you won the number of pence shown on the square, but the coin almost always came to rest on one of the intersecting lines and you just lost your penny); you could also knock down coconuts, shoot the heads off moving cardboard ducks or clowns and throw rubber rings over the prizes on show - although anything of any real value was perched on the back row, well out of reach of even the most skilled contenders, who were usually at best presented with a bowl of goldfishes.

One stall attracted me particularly. A large panel at its centre was divided into several oblong sections, each showing the name of a town. When players pressed their electric push buttons a light moved up and down until it came to rest on one of the names eventually. After carefully assessing the prizes on view - big cuddly toys, canteens of cutlery, tennis racquets and sets of saucepans and so on - Maureen and I invested our sixpences and, when the light stopped on my BLACKPOOL, I nearly deafened everybody with my tremendous shout of, "Here!" I was deflated completely when the stall attendant handed me a small rubber elephant from a pile of cheap toys which I hadn't even noticed.

"Oh, no - I want the knives and forks!" I stammered protestingly and Maureen nodded emphatically in agreement.

"Naw - you 'ave to win three times for one of them big prizes," was the man's unsympathetic but adamant response. "Take this or you get nothing!"

Reckoning swiftly that I had only just enough money left for a last float in the swingboat, I accepted the elephant disdainfully and Maureen and I dashed off to warn our pals to keep away from that particular stall.

There were two more local annual events in November. Bonfire Night was anticipated with great excitement. For weeks in advance of 5th November we collected old furniture, odd pieces of wood, tree and hedge prunings and anything else combustible from people in the neighbourhood and stacked it all into a pile on the waste ground between Highfield and Churchfield Terraces. As the mound grew we formed a rota to keep watch on the collection, as it was liable to be raided by gangs of youngsters from other districts. Dad used to set off a few fireworks in the backyard at No. 12 immediately after tea and then I'd nip round quickly to watch Dorothy's affluent display of giant pinwheels, coloured fairy fountains, snow-storms and rockets. Afterwards we would munch her mother's home-made treacle toffee around the bonfire until the guy had gone up in flames. The next morning Maureen and I always held a postmortem at the site and often found the remaining black ashes still smouldering. Fred was frequently kept indoors for a couple of days as punishment for being accused unfairly of throwing lighted rip-raps into neighbours' letter boxes.

In contrast, the commemoration of the 1918 Armistice was a sombre affair. A two minutes' silence was observed at precisely 11am on whatever day 11th November fell in the current year. If we were in school at the time we had to stand up in readiness at five to eleven and were ordered to remain completely still and silent during the requisite period - marked at the beginning and end by a distant piercing factory hooter. It was amazing how many pupils seemed to find they needed to cough or clear their throats just before eleven o'clock. At home and elsewhere everyone used to stop whatever they were doing as soon as the hooter sounded and observe the silence obedi-ently.

On the Sunday before 11th November, members of the British Legion, various other organisations and local dignitar-ies formed a procession (usually led by the Salvation Army band) and walked to the local cenotaph, where war veterans and relatives of some of the men who'd been killed in action laid poppy wreaths. At the head of them marched Todger Jones, a Runcornian who had been awarded the Victoria Cross for bravery in the war, and during the ceremony everyone sang, "O God, our help in ages past".

Parliamentary Elections were preceded by a good deal of political activity. Posters advertising the professed aims of the three parties concerned were plastered around the town and the candidates, wearing big coloured rosettes (at that time red for Conservatives, blue for Liberal and yellow for Labour) canvassed outside factories and offices during lunch-breaks and at other times held open-air and indoor meetings all over the place.

Runcorn had been part of a Conservative stronghold for a number of years, but keener interest among the growing labour force in the chemical works and tanneries was beginning to cause a swing to the left and as a result rivalry had intensified. Up to then the majority of local people had had little real knowledge of politics and had voted unquestioningly in accordance with the family precedent, but their newly-adult offspring were beginning to challenge old views and weren't afraid of expressing individual opinions publicly. Consequently heckling at the meetings often became really fierce and one night Maureen and I joined a crowd of mixed allegiances in the centre of the town, hoping fervently that things might get out of hand and perhaps even finish up with a fight.

Soon after we arrived on the scene two of the candidates, Lord Crichton-Stuart (Conservative) and one representing the Labour party, decided to abandon a personal argument in which neither seemed to get the better of the other, and which had proved to be disappointingly unprovocative to bystanders. The ensuing brief lull in the proceedings was broken suddenly by a lusty call from a man near the front of the crowd: "Why don't you both take a leaf out of Mr Asquith's book?" and I realised with horror that it had come from Uncle Peter.

After a moment's puzzled silence the Conservative candidate repeated politely, "Mr Asquith's book, sir? I'm afraid I don't quite follow..."

"Do what Mr Asquith said we should always do - wait and see!" Uncle Peter demanded fiercely. Lord Crichton-Stuart and his opponent muttered together for a minute and, as no-one else appeared to support the suggestion, evidently agreed that it was too vague to be pursued. I breathed a sigh of relief when another voice asked petulantly to be told which one of the parties intended to give more money to farm workers and Uncle Peter stalked away in disgust.

"What did your Uncle Peter mean - telling them to wait and see, like Mr Asquith?" Maureen queried on our way home.

"I don't know," I answered crossly. "I only wish he'd kept his mouth shut!" Then family loyalty came to the fore.

"He does read a lot about politics in the papers and Pearson's Weekly though," I defended, "and I bet not many people who were at that meeting tonight had ever even heard of Mr Asquith!" At least that silenced Maureen, who certainly had not.

A couple of weeks before that particular election we heard that each of the three contesting parties were looking for youngsters to act as "runners" on voting day. Our informer didn't know whether there would be any payment for the service but was definitely sure that free refreshments would be provided at the respective committee rooms.

"Let's go to the Labour place in High Street," suggested Maureen. "My Dad's going to vote for them."

I contemplated the situation more shrewdly.

"No - we'll do better with the Conservatives," I decided. "They've got plenty of money, so their refreshments should be nicer."

So, in spite of the fact that her parents were voting Labour and mine Liberal, we stood together outside the polling station at Halton Road Church on election day bedecked with red rosettes and politely asked voters for their electoral register numbers. Every couple of hours we dashed to the nearest Conservative committee rooms with our lists, so that party officials could round up any dilatory supporters before the poll closed and, on each trip, we helped ourselves liberally to the lavish refreshments on offer.

Most people gave their register numbers willingly enough, but one old lady turned on Maureen angrily. "This is supposed to be a secret ballot," she stormed, "and I'm not going to tell you or anyone else what my number is!"

"Stuck-up, toffee-nosed old faggot!" Maureen snarled at the woman's retreating back and then, forgetting her own temporary affiliation added, "Bet she's rubbishy Conservative, too!"

We Brays never once had a family holiday away from home but were treated to odd days out during Dad's annual week off from the tannery. These were usually trips by bus or train (with a very early start so that Mother and Dad could get their own tickets at the cheap workman's rate) to New Brighton, Rhyl or Blackpool and the highlight of the day was a fish-and-chips meal in a promenade cafe.

In the hope of increasing sales during summer months just then, the "News Chronicle" engaged a mystery man known as Lobby Lud to visit seaside resorts in various parts of the country and offered a reward of £10 to any reader who correctly recognised him. His whereabouts for the forthcoming week were published in the Saturday's paper, together with a rather sinister photograph showing a side view of him wearing a trilby hat but revealing little of his actual features. When a holiday outing was planned for us, I used to beg for it to be to one of Lobby Lud's scheduled ports of call and then spent the day prowling around the resort on my own with a copy of the newspaper tucked under my arm as specified, peering suspiciously at all men in trilby hats and frequently pouncing on one with the required challenge: "You are Mr Lobby Lud - I claim the "News Chronicle" prize!" My accusations often caused amusement and sometimes annoyance, but I was never smart enough to corner the elusive quarry, although when details of his capture were published in the following day's newspaper I invariably managed to convince myself that I must have been very close to him just about the time he'd been correctly spotted!

# Chapter 8

The majority of what were to me the most memorable events of my childhood were connected with Halton Road Wesleyan Methodist Church.

I enrolled as a member of the primary department there just before my fourth birthday. The sessions were held every Sunday afternoon in a sunny room furnished with tiny chairs and a piano, and were under the direction of two spinster sisters, Miss Ada and Miss Mary. The latter were middle-aged but by no means frumpish; they always wore high-heeled shoes and brightly coloured clothes and I remember I was very puzzled at one time because their hair suddenly changed colour from grey tinted with blue to ginger, which in retrospect I think might have coincided with the arrival of a new, unmarried minister at the church. Miss Mary played the piano and Miss Ada helped us to sing verses from "Gentle Jesus, meek and mild" and "All things bright and beautiful" and, on one momentous occasion, another little girl and myself were made to stand in opposite corners of the room, each holding a lighted candle while the others sang:

"Jesus bids us shine with a pure, clear light
 Like a little candle burning in the night;
 Through the darkness we may shine,
 You in your small corner and I in mine."

We also recited the Lord's prayer each week and our teachers took turns reading out a passage from the Bible. I always thought Miss Mary was the best at that, especially when she did the Ten Commandments and banged her fist on top of the piano at the end of every one of them.

The atmosphere in the primary school was very cosy and Jesus, holding a lamb and a shepherd's crook, smiled down at us from a big picture on the wall. I believed that the halo shining above his head was a full moon which must have helped a lot while he was busy looking for the little lamb. The sisters told us that he loved us and I felt I liked him too, because he had nice, kind eyes and seemed to be fond of animals as well. At that stage, however, I was not so happy about the fearsome God who was apparently waiting somewhere out of sight if I did anything wrong and I always behaved myself very well for at least a few hours after I'd heard him mentioned. I was mystified completely by any reference to a Holy Ghost and tried not to think about that at all.

After two years in the primary school department I moved up into the main Sunday School, which accommodated children up to about the age of fourteen. There we used to sit on forms in the centre of the hall at the start of the service at two o'clock (boys on one side, girls on the other); the Superintendent said prayers and we sang hymns before splitting up into classes for lessons from teachers. Attendances were recorded weekly by a registrar, who rubber-stamped star symbols on our individual "star cards". If you missed a Sunday because of sickness or holidays you had to take along an explanatory note from your parents and he'd stamp your card with a special "S" or "H" symbol for those dates. At the end of each year first and second class book prizes were awarded for good attendance.

Once a year there was a special service in aid of Foreign Missions, when a missionary visited the church to describe his work overseas and we lustily sang the hymns, "From Greenland's icy mountains to India's coral strand..." and "Wide, wide as the ocean..." Young volunteer collectors were given sealed wooden boxes (with a picture of little coloured children on one side) to be filled at home with money for the cause and, on return of them, beribboned medals were presented to anyone who'd managed to collect three pounds or over, with bars added to the medals for similar success in further years. At Halton Road the most prominent collector was Lizzie, a cripple in a wheelchair, who had a whole row of medals and bars pinned across her chest. I remember that Mother was annoyed when on one occasion both Fred and I eagerly accepted collecting boxes; we were sent swiftly to beg for supportive offerings from relatives, but unfortunately these didn't continue beyond initial subscriptions and in spite of trying to persuade Dad and Uncle Peter to top up the boxes on the day we were due to return them, neither of us earned a medal.

On Sundays I wore a pinafore immediately I got home from Sunday School and tea at No. 12 was a special affair. A starched white damask cloth covered the table and the best crockery and cutlery were brought out (most of the latter had been acquired, like my doll from Aunt Emma, by the collection of soap packet coupons). The meal was always either cold meat or tinned salmon, followed by stewed or tinned fruit with custard and Grandma's currant cake; as soon as it was over the white cloth was replaced for the rest of the day by a heavy, dark one with tassels round the edges.

The main event on the Sunday School calendar was the Anniversary Service, which was held in the main chapel upstairs on the second Sunday in May. The chapel was arena-shaped, with sloping rows of wooden pews (a few of which were "rented" by better-off devotees and fitted with red plush cushions), intersecting aisles and an altar rail and raised pulpit with choir stalls and organ behind it at the far end. The organ pipes reached almost to the ceiling, which was festooned with clusters of flowers and angels painted in blue and gold, and stained glass windows were set high in the walls on three sides. For several weeks before the Anniversary, scholars used to practise songs and recitations for the morning, afternoon and evening services. I was always chosen to recite and when I stood up to do so used to fix my eyes intently on a dove in the centre of one of the stained glass windows, so that I could forget the terrifying sea of faces in front of me and concentrate on my lines.

The afternoon service was usually based on a religious theme of some sort. For instance, one year it was entitled "The Building of the Church"; scholars sang the hymn, "The Church's one foundation..." at the beginning and "For all the saints who from their labour rest..." at the end and, in between, each of us laid a counterfeit brick behind the altar rail and said a few words to indicate that it represented one of the various attributes upon which the Church of Christ had been built. Perhaps appropriately, Dorothy laid a brick for "The Beauty of Godliness", Maureen for "Perseverance in Adversity" and mine was for "Willing Labour."

It was customary for a local dignitary to preside over the afternoon's proceedings and give a short (or sometimes interminably long and boring) address, and one day the wife of the chairman of the Town Council surprised us by saying at the end of hers that she would give a prize to the scholar who wrote out the best account of what she had talked about. Amazingly, I'd been listening fairly attentively and was able to send in a reasonably accurate effort in my best handwriting: Maureen hadn't, but persuaded me to scribble a different version for her to copy out. A couple of weeks later the Sunday School Superintendent announced that, as the lady had been unable to decide which was the better of two of the many entries - mine or Maureen's - she had sent a prize for each of us. Maureen never even blushed as we went on to the platform to receive them, but I'm afraid I should definitely not have behaved in a very Christian-like manner if she'd been awarded the only prize!

Adult members of our and other churches used to flock to the Anniversary performances and there was always a particularly good attendance in the evenings, when extra seating accommodation had to be provided by putting wooden forms and chairs along the aisles. Quite often the hymn-singing then became so ardent that the organist would abandon his accompaniment because the congregation drowned it completely. Right at the end of the service there was an expectant minute's silence before the minister named the total sum obtained from the collections taken during the day for the benefit of Sunday School funds. Similar services were held at the other Methodist Churches in turn throughout the early summer and Maureen and I often went to them, mainly in order to compare (always adversely!) the performance of their scholars with our own.

Anniversaries at churches in the Runcorn circuit used to increase trade in shops in the town. Most boys and girls wore a new outfit on the day and we Brays were no exception. Towards the end of April, frilly muslin dresses, straw hats, fancy socks and gloves were displayed in local traders' windows; some of my pals could boast about their new apparel a couple of weeks in advance, but Mother always took us to be fitted up after Dad had received his wage packet on the Friday evening before Halton Road's turn.

My outfit usually consisted of one of Beth's dresses cut down to size, a new pair of Clarks sandals and a Panama hat (held on by a strip of elastic under my chin) which I could use for school later and, of course, I used to grumble that Dorothy's patent leather ankle-strap slippers and straw bonnet with rosebuds and ribbon streamers looked much nicer. Once Maureen secretly borrowed a hat from her sister's collection - a wide-brimmed creation with an ostrich feather drooping at the side, which so incensed the Superintendent that he ordered her to sit as inconspicuously as possible on the back row of the forms allocated to Sunday School scholars. Fred was rigged out in grey flannel trousers, a blazer and cream silk shirt, but his friends often played truant on the day and spent their triple batches of collection money on sweets. Older members of the church also used to give their summer attire a first showing at the Anniversary services; the two spinster sisters who ran the primary department - and were also members of the church choir - were always much in evidence in flamboyant dresses and big picture hats.

At the beginning of December we had a Christmas bazaar, with stalls laden with home-made cakes, jams and pickles, treacle toffee and fudge (which Maureen and I thought were priced extortionately) and piles of garments hand-embroidered by ladies of the Mothers' Union. There were raffles for guessing the name of a doll, the weight of a cake, or the number of dried peas in a jar, and Sunday School teachers trotted around in fancy aprons, busily serving refreshments.

One year Dorothy, dressed as a fairy in billowing white tulle and a tinsel wreath on top of her long curls, sat on the platform by the side of a large tub labelled "Lucky Dip". After you'd paid sixpence she waved the wand above the tub and you drew a surprise packet out of it. Unwilling to acknowledge that I wasn't nearly so decorative as my playmate, I felt very bitter that she and not I had been chosen to wave the wand. "Especially," I pointed out plaintively to Maureen, "as I'm always a first-class attender at Sunday School and she hardly ever gets even a second-class prize!" "I think they've picked her because of her ringlets," Maureen consoled after a quick glance at my hair, which at that time was cut into an Eton crop because Mother's bun and Beth's plaits never necessitated a trip to the hairdresser and I had to be sent along to the barber's with Dad and Fred.

At Harvest Festival window ledges in the main chapel were bedecked with sheaves of corn alongside flowers, fruit and vegetables of almost every description and scholars lined up to heap individual gifts behind the altar rail. The following evening vegetables were auctioned to raise money for church funds, the flowers and fruit were distributed to sick people and we had a Harvest supper of hotpot and pickled red cabbage in the Sunday School room.

A Band of Hope meeting was held on one evening of every week throughout the year. Its aim was to discourage the consumption of alcohol; members were given a large blue ribbon to pin on to their coats as proof that they'd signed a pledge of non-indulgence, and thereafter were called "Blue Ribboners". Perhaps I was rather young to make such a drastic decision, but at the age of seven I went along to join in and obligingly signed the pledge - actually with the sole intent of acquiring a ribbon!

An instance of combined religious activity was the annual Whit Monday procession through the town. Clergy, church members and Sunday School scholars of all denominations first assembled at their own place of worship behind banners displaying biblical illustrations and the name of their church. The banners were hung on poles and carried by church officials and streamers spreading out from them were held by some of the older scholars. Other scholars, teachers and a few church members walked behind and very young children were transported on lorries or on carts pulled by horses sporting plaited manes, brasses and huge coloured rosettes. (Fred used to flatly refuse to join the walkers and could always be seen seated comfortably on one of the lorries, albeit in the course of time head and shoulders above his companions). By degrees the various contingents combined into a single formation and, headed by a brass or silver band, marched through the main streets to Runcorn Heath. Townspeople used to hang out of bedroom windows or line the pavements to watch, waving to friends and relations taking part. I never once knew the proceedings to be abandoned nor even postponed because of bad weather and sometimes it was so hot that the tar on the roads melted and stuck to our plimsolls. At the end of the journey the procession disbanded and there were immediate long queues for ice-cream and pop. By prior arrangement all local members of the early Webster clan and their offspring gathered near to the water tower and were treated to ice-creams by Uncle Peter. After about an hour on the Heath, church parties re-assembled and marched back to their various Sunday School rooms for a tea of ham sandwiches and seed cake.

Although some Roman Catholics joined in with the Whit Monday walk they also had a separate parade (usually on the Sunday before Whitsun weekend), when little girls were dressed in white dresses and veils, teenage girls in the blue capes of the Legion of Mary and men wore the red sashes of the Knights of St Columba. Their procession was quite short and went from their own day school to the Catholic Church.

In summer, Halton Road scholars were given a free Saturday afternoon outing by bus to Frodsham Hill (about six miles from Runcorn). Headed by Maureen, a little gang of us used to push our way on to the first of the buses to make sure of bagging seats at the back and then wound down the windows and waved and yelled at people on the pavements all the way to Frodsham. At the top of the hill there were swings and a helter-skelter and long wooden sheds in which we queued for refreshment. One year Maureen and I got two helpings by joining the queue twice over and would probably have managed more if we hadn't been spotted by one of the teachers. The

*Annual Sunday School Trip Day - Frodsham Hill.*

Sunday School officials organised races for us on the grassy slopes but, after making sure that we'd received at least our due quota of currant buns and lemonade and decided that the prizes on offer to winners were not really worth the necessary effort, Maureen and I always preferred to wander off on our own.

The sprawling gorse bushes and tall matted ferns on Frodsham's hillside made a marvellous rambling ground and, on one outing, the two of us caused great consternation by re-appearing in a dishevelled state long after the buses were due to leave for home. Just as our teacher was about to scold us severely, Maureen looked up at her piously and said, "We got lost, Miss Moores, but we knelt down and prayed to Jesus and He's brought us back safely," and we each received a pat on the head instead!

# Chapter 9

In the 1930's pupils at primary schools in Cheshire were segregated between the ages of ten and twelve for further education at either Grammar type or secondary schools. The curriculum at the secondary schools did not include higher mathematics, foreign languages nor science subjects, but aimed at a good standard of education in general subjects and tuition in specialised crafts such as wood and metal work, dressmaking and typewriting.

Most children living on the Cheshire side of the River Mersey and within approximately eight miles of Runcorn progressed to either the local County Grammar School in Waterloo Road or to one of the several alternative secondary schools in the district. Some townsfolk (notably doctors and the like) paid for family education to be continued at Liverpool College in Mossley Hill or the King's/Queen's School in Chester and a small private establishment run by two Quaker sisters catered for some others between the ages of five and sixteen. Catholics had their own school for infants and primary pupils, who later either made use of the County Council facilities or were sent on to senior Catholic schools and colleges in other towns.

Each year a number of scholarships for free tuition at the Runcorn Grammar School were awarded to boys and girls of requisite age - about ten by the County Education Committee, one by the Co-operative Wholesale Society and one by the Highfield Tanning Company. All the awards were based on the results of open examinations, but competition for the CWS place was restricted to the offspring of Society members, and for the Tannery one to sons and daughters of employees there. The remainder of the places at the Grammar School were filled by the children of fairly affluent parents, who enrolled them as fee-paying (or "private") scholars at a charge of £3 per term plus the cost of text books etc. A few youngsters with convenient dates of birth resorted to the practice of attending as private pupils for one year and, as they could still compete for a free place within the specified age limits the following year, they were thus assured of being able to continue the better standard of education either way. Needless to say, none of the barge children ever moved into the higher sphere.

A year before Beth was eligible to sit the examination for entry to the Grammar School, Dad bought ten volumes of encyclopedias from a man at the door, with a view to improving her general knowledge in readiness but, after several months' intensive cramming, her nervous condition worsened. She did not win a scholarship and duly transferred from Victoria Road to the Balfour Road School for Girls. Dad decided that Fred and I were too young to learn anything from the books and they were stored away on the top shelf of a bookcase in the parlour, well out of reach. I remember standing on tiptoe on a chair once and dragging one of them down in hope of finding out more about coal mining, which we had been studying at school and I thought might be included in test questions scheduled for the following day. From the binder containing a brief paragraph on "Coal" I was referred in turn to "Fuel Supplies", "Gas Manufacture", "Lancashire Coalfields" and "Tar Production". Each snippet was of course in a separate volume; I was soon infuriated and indeed exhausted by lifting them all down and up again and abandoned the search altogether when I found that the illustrated bit about "Wild Flowers", just ahead of "Worsley Seams" was far more interesting anyway.

When I was ten the headmistress at Victoria Road School recommended that I should compete that year at both the County and the Tanning Company examinations. I received no parental encouragement whatever - in fact, my mention of the scholarships at home inexplicably brought on another of Dad's sulks and Mother, of course, was always far too busy with household chores to involve herself in anything more than my general physical well-being. All the same, I added my name to the two lists of competitors.

The tests for the place to be awarded to a child of an employee of the tannery came first and were held one Saturday in the Highfield Institute - a single storey building on the outskirts of the town, normally used for the firm's social activities. A few candidates (including myself) weren't tall enough to reach up to the clothes hooks in the cloakroom there and had to leave our coats on top of one of the billiard tables before we sat down on collapsible chairs at baize-topped whist tables. During the morning session we completed papers in Arithmetic and English Grammar; in the afternoon there were questions on General Knowledge and we had to write an essay from a choice of four subjects. I caused a slight disturbance at the beginning of the first session because the nib of the pen I'd been supplied with was faulty; apparently such a contingency hadn't been envisaged and no spares were to hand, but one of the two gentlemen invigilating at the proceedings kindly offered to lend me his fountain pen, which I accepted with delighted alacrity, although I'd never used one before. Fortunately it didn't run dry on me.

At lunchtime sandwiches and hot and cold drinks were laid on in the canteen but we weren't allowed to leave the building. In between tests I tried to assess the ability of my fellow competitors; I knew most of them and decided that either a girl who went to the Quaker sisters' private school or a boy from Victoria Road who had been specially coached at home for the exam stood the best chances of success. Amongst other pen-nibblers around me were three boys and two girls who were quite a bit older than me and had been at the Grammar School on a fee-paying basis for almost a year already. One of the boys, wearing large horn-rimmed spectacles, a bow-tie and his Grammar School blazer, looked as if he might be very clever. However, I felt reasonably confident that I could at least match Dorothy Dawson's performance, even though she was dressed magnificently in pale pink with the usual satin ribbons in her hair. I was in the clothes I'd worn for school throughout the previous week, apart from a clean pair of long woollen stockings which made my legs itch unbearably all day.

As we came out of the Institute together at half past three, Dorothy asked eagerly, "How did you get on?"

"Not bad," I replied ungrammatically, "but I'm glad it's over." Actually my only real concern was to get home quickly so that I could peel off my itchy stockings.

"Oh, I thought it was all very easy - especially the sums," she went on. "I got through nearly all the mental arithmetic and I really enjoyed doing the problem about the man going off on holiday. How long did you work out it took his train to go from Bristol to Plymouth?"

I shrugged my shoulders and hazarded vaguely, "Something like three and a quarter hours, I think." Dorothy was immediately elated.

"Then you were wrong on that one," she cried triumphantly, "because Jack Nelson said the same as me - five hours! You mustn't have noticed that it broke down just outside Exeter." I felt sure I had in fact allowed for the stoppage, but seemingly Jack Nelson was the lad with the bow-tie and it was unlikely that he could have got it wrong.

"Well, I couldn't care less," I lied, kicking aggressively at a pebble on the pavement, and added peevishly, "Who wants to go to Plymouth for a holiday anyway?"

The examinations for the free places to be given by the Education Authority were held a couple of weeks later in primary schools attended currently by competitors. Maureen's father didn't work at the Tannery but she was eligible to try for one of the County scholarships. On the day of the examination she raided the pantry at home early in the morning, swallowed six Oxo cubes and a cupful of salted water to make herself sick, and easily convinced her mother that she was too ill to even leave the house.

One Saturday morning a few weeks later she and I were attempting to knock conkers off each other's strings on the grass patch at the side of No. 12 when a man from the Tannery office pulled up in his car and knocked at the front door. After he'd driven off again Dad beckoned me into the lobby and without any show of excitement whatever announced, "You've won the Tannery scholarship." My immediate glow of satisfaction was dampened by his apparent lack of interest and, for a couple of seconds, I was afraid he might start up yet another sulk, but he didn't and I think the result must actually have given him a little pleasure, because when he received a letter from Chester the following week offering me a County scholarship place he said gruffly, "You'll have to turn this down and accept the one from the firm. That way I'll get a feather in my cap, too."

Mother seemed to be quite pleased by my success and Uncle Peter volunteered to buy a second-hand bicycle for me as a reward, but Grandma was not happy at all to hear the news.

"You'll be like a monkey on a stick now and the higher up you go the further you'll have to come sliding down!" she forecast dismally. I didn't realise then that she would be repeating that particular prophecy to me for a number of years to come! Dorothy's parents were somewhat dismayed when they heard of my achievement and, not to be outdone, they enrolled her as a private pupil at the Grammar School.

And so I parted company from the majority of my old friends at Vicky Road (as Maureen and I had always called it affectionately) and at the beginning of September that year continued my education in fresh pastures.

# Chapter 10

The Runcorn County Grammar School (originally the local Technical Institute) had been built in Waterloo Road in 1894. It was approached from the front by a flight of thirteen stone steps and heavy swing doors at the top of them led into a wide entrance hall. The ground floor housed the headmaster's study and a small staff room, the gymnasium, physics laboratory, boys' cloakroom and three large classrooms and a staircase went up from the hall to the girls' cloakroom, cookery kitchen, chemistry laboratory and more classrooms. Most of the rooms were separated by sliding wood and glass partitions and the Art room had very large windows. There was also a side entrance leading to a yard at the back, where cycles could be stored. Most pupils went home for midday meals but those who lived out of town ate packed lunches under supervision in the woodwork section in the basement - there was no canteen.

School uniform was compulsory; girls wore gymslips, white blouses with striped ties, navy gabardine coats and velour hats in winter and pink-checked print dresses, blazers and Panama hats in summer. Boys wore white shirts, short or long grey flannels, blazers and caps. I was extremely proud of my new leather satchel with my initials stamped on the front (rather surprisingly not supplied by the tannery), but rather dismayed to learn that scholarship holders had to hand down some of their textbooks year by year. The second-hand ones I inherited when I started at the school were in a very tatty condition and I had to piece them together with paste and cover them painstakingly with brown paper to stop them dropping to bits.

Forms were split into A and B sections in separate rooms, each section consisting of 30/40 boys and girls and the masters and mistresses (dressed in long black gowns and mortar boards) taught individual subjects. I started off in 1A and was greatly relieved to see that Dorothy had been assigned to 1B.

My favourite subject was English, taught by a middle-aged spinster with an extremely strident voice who would have needed no disguise whatsoever to portray one of the witches in "Macbeth". She wore her mortarboard at a slightly tipsy angle and her frequent raucous demands of, "Is this a dagger that I see before me?" and "Romeo, Romeo, wherefore art thou, Romeo?" penetrated piercingly through the glass partition separating our class from the one next door. The boys used to snigger when she delivered Juliet's sugary sentiments, but she inspired me tremendously; she had wonderful knowledge of English Grammar and Literature and struggled hard to pass on to us her own art of clear expression and precise detail on paper. "I'll not be judging the size of your buns," she would warn prior to essay writing, "- just the number of currants they contain!"

Drawing lessons had been infrequent at Victoria Road, but I now surprisingly produced a belated talent in Art, for which the master was a little Belgian who remarked consistently to anyone he caught yawning, "I just saw the tail of the kipper you had for breakfast!" In addition to giving us rather boring instruction on sketching inanimate objects he placed on a stool in the centre of the room, he tried to stimulate our artistic imagination by sometimes quoting a few lines from a book or poem and telling us to demonstrate them in picture form. On one occasion he loudly praised my interpretation of, "I remember, I remember the house where I was born..." and to my great delight hung it on the wall in the Art room. It depicted a dark stone mansion with lots of latticed windows, but in truth the stately home and its surrounding "pine trees dark and high" could in no way be likened to No. 12 Highfield Terrace and nearby tannery chimneys.

I enjoyed my initiation into Maths, Chemistry, Physics and French and furthering my knowledge of History and Geography, but took instant dislike to Latin, chiefly due to an antipathy to the tutor for that subject. During 1A's very first lesson with him he announced that he intended to translate our surnames into their Latin equivalents and address us accordingly thereafter. After acknowledging that the nearest he could get to Bray was by associating my name with a donkey's bray, he decided that I should be dubbed "Asina" - the Latin equivalent for a female donkey. To my extreme humiliation, the rest of the form found that hilarious and my annoyance must have been very obvious to both them and the master. "Sulking, are you?" he demanded when I refused stubbornly to answer to my new name at the next lesson. "Right - if you're incapable of assimilating anything but English, you'll be known simply as "Donkey" in the future!" And as such I remained to him for the rest of our acquaintance, even though he reverted swiftly enough to addressing my classmates by their normal surnames. His antagonistic attitude in another instance did in fact cause a really brainy lad to drop the subject altogether and discover at a later date that a lack of proficiency in it barred him from applying for entry to Oxford and Cambridge Universities.

I was greatly relieved to find that needlework was not included in the school curriculum, but the profiteroles and meringues I made in the cookery class were as unsuccessful as my previous attempts at anything connected even remotely with domesticity. They were not improved, of course, by being jogged home on the carrier at  the rear of my second-hand bicycle. "Why can't they show you how to make a tasty meat pie instead of this rubbish?" Grandma used to ask petulantly and Mother usually grumbled about the cost of the ingredients I had to take along for such extravagant items - which only Uncle Peter, with his customary scorn of waste, was ever willing to consume.

There were no music lessons at the Grammar School, but a few periods were set aside from time to time for practising songs and carols so that pupils could be chosen to sing in the school choir on special occasions. I was always asked politely but very quickly to remove myself from the contenders. I discovered, however, that my much-detested Latin master was an accomplished violinist and had formed a class outside set hours for the benefit of anyone who wished to learn to play the instrument. On hearing this, I decided to shelve my dislike of him temporarily because Uncle Peter possessed an old violin which he'd bought from a shipmate who'd been desperate to lay hands on cash at some time. It had never been used but I borrowed it and joined the school group enthusiastically.

Unfortunately my initiation into the art of playing the fiddle chanced to come only a few days before a Parents' Evening at which musical items, etc were to be executed. New members of the violin class, including myself, were obviously incapable of making any worthwhile contribution to the performance of practised budding artistes but, in an effort to swell the number of boys and girls on the platform on the night, we were told to stand inconspicuously in the back row and move our bows up and down in imitation of the players' strokes - without actually touching the strings. All went well with the piece until for some unknown reason my concentration lapsed and during what should have been a brief pause in the score my bow descended awkwardly and gave out an agonising screech.

At the end of the performance I left the platform with the rest of the players and sat through an ensuing display of gymnastics until it was time for everyone to leave. Anticipating the wrath of the Latin/Music master, I planned to slip out of the room swiftly but, to my horror, saw that he was standing close to the only exit. When he caught sight of me the pleasant smile he'd been distributing to parents congratulating him on the competence of his pupils vanished instantly and, in a voice necessarily subdued by their proximity, he hissed, "Donkey - here!" I stopped meekly in front of him, hugging my violin.

"You did that deliberately, didn't you?" he accused, glaring at me and rubbing the end of his nose ominously. I recollected that my Sunday School teachers always reckoned that honesty was the best policy in such a situation.

"No sir, I didn't!" I denied truthfully. "I don't know what happened exactly - I think my bow just caught the strings. I-I'm very sorry."

"Sorry!" he repeated furiously. "I should think you are! I hope you realise that you spoiled our evening completely? You should be downright ashamed of yourself!"

Fortunately for me, another cluster of parents moved towards the door just then and his baleful glare was replaced by a beaming smile once more as he extended his hand to one of them. I sidled out quickly. The next day he told me coldly that he'd deleted the name of "Donkey" from his list of aspiring musicians and, to my chagrin, the violin had to be returned without further ado to its former seclusion underneath Peter's bed.

Physical training was enforced for one hour once a week in the gymnasium; there were no outside sports facilities at the school premises but pupils had the use of a large field and pavilion about a mile and a half away. We had to make our own way to it and also supply all individual playing equipment, although tennis courts and football and hockey goalposts were in situ and a groundsman was employed to attend to the site. I liked hockey best and was soon promoted to the Second XI. My usual position for play was left inside - I secretly coveted that of centre forward but it was allocated consistently to a girl in an upper form who stood head and shoulders above even the games mistress and was almost as wide as she was tall; when she was in motion her hair flew out in all directions and on wintry days her bared knees resembled huge pieces of raw beef. Her size and aggressiveness intimidated opponents into distancing themselves to safety when they saw her charging up the field; she was aptly nicknamed "Bessie Bunter" and, in deference to her superiority in the game, the rest of us would stand by meekly while she demolished most of the lemon slices distributed at half time during matches.

Although I settled into the new curriculum fairly quickly, it didn't take me long to deduce that demarcation between most private pupils and scholarship holders in my form was not measured solely by standards of academic achievement. Boys and girls who'd been given free places usually headed the exam results, but I felt that scholastic success seemed to be of secondary importance to the inability to "keep up with the Joneses" in the classrooms in other respects. Most of the private pupils lived in the most salubrious district of Runcorn and quite a few of them looked down their noses at "scholarship kids."

Some pupils could boast of the advantage of a room set aside for study at home. Each of my three fee-paying cousins did, but I had to do my homework at No. 12 kneeling on a chair at the side of our newly-acquired gramophone cabinet, because the table was rarely cleared before ten o'clock at night in case Uncle Peter appeared for a late meal. Oftener than not the wireless set was blaring away in the background, the volume turned up high to allow for Dad's deafness. I couldn't use the parlour as Beth had started to take piano forte lessons and was practising the scales in there every evening: although I wasn't so unfortunate as Danny White, the CWS scholarship boy - he came from a very poor family and was compelled to study on the stairs at home out of range of his eight brothers and sisters. Neither his parents nor mine ever came to a Parents' Evening or Prize-giving (he was brilliantly clever and won at least one prize every year) but, in fairness to Mother and Dad, I must admit that, owing to my exaggerated concern over what I considered our hapless social position, I never encouraged them to do so.

Fortunately, teaching staff didn't share the snobbishness adopted by some of my form-mates and assessed us all on standards of academic achievement and behaviour only, but that didn't prevent me from developing an inferiority complex and, as a result, I was never really happy in my new environment. In fact, I wished quite frequently that I'd taken the same less ambitious path of learning as my old pal Maureen who, after transferring to Balfour Road Girls' School had apparently plunged into a variety of exciting outside interests and already acquired a host of youthful male admirers.

# Chapter 11

Like Maureen, most of my former classmates at Victoria Road
had gone on to Balfour Road School, and none of the three who
had won County Scholarships lived near me. Dorothy stayed in
the B stream and I spent only brief spells with her, mostly at
events connected with Halton Road Sunday School, which we
both still attended. Consequently I was more or less left on my
own outside school hours in my first year, but during the second
became friendly with Eve Halligan-Simms, with whom I then
shared equipment in the cookery class.

She was a pretty, delicately-featured girl, rather like a
porcelain doll. She had huge brown eyes and fair, curly hair and
was always extremely ladylike, with the natural manners of
someone who always knew how to behave correctly without
having to think first. Her school blouses were made of pure silk
and she coated her neatly-trimmed finger and toe nails with
expensive pearl varnish. She was, of course, at the school on a
fee-paying basis but I was the only fellow pupil in 2A whose
home was in the immediate neighbourhood of hers.

Eve lived off Halton Road with Major and Mrs Pedlow, her
uncle and aunt, in "Birchwood", a house whose dimensions were
unique in that vicinity. It looked Georgian and was surrounded
by spacious grounds and a high wall. Her father worked abroad
- or at least travelled to the Orient frequently - and he used to
bring gifts of kimonos and painted fans and parasols for her
whenever he paid one of his rare visits to Runcorn. She never
mentioned her mother; I once asked if she was dead but Eve
replied, "No," abruptly and started to talk about something else

straight away. It didn't occur to me that her parents may have been divorced - such a circumstance was very uncommon in those days and usually only associated vaguely with American film stars and other celebrities, so I remained mystified.

I abandoned the use of my bicycle in favour of walking to school with my new friend, and used to make an early morning call at "Birchwood" on weekdays, mounting wide stone steps and standing on tiptoe to pull the bell-rope alongside the massive front door. A maid wearing a black dress and white starched apron and cap always let me in and in broken English used to ask me gutturally to, "Kindly enter and come for to wait in the library." My steel-tipped brogues clanged embarrassingly on the mosaic tiles every time I crossed the hall.

The library was a huge room with two bay windows overlooking the orchard, and housed scores of leather-bound volumes on shelves reaching to the ceiling on three sides. There were ornate Chinese rugs on the floor, subdued wall lights and a tall, glass-fronted cabinet filled with lots of little pieces of china, jade and ivory. I used to perch on the very edge of what I was sure must have been a genuine Chippendale chair so that I could turn around easily to view all the exhibits, and I never minded how long I had to wait before Eve was ready to set off for school. On her birthday I was invited to tea in the dining-room. It contained a big oval table (around which at least eight people could have been seated comfortably), and with a highly-polished surface reflecting two massive glass chandeliers hanging from the ceiling. A long sideboard made in the same wood and adorned with carved fruit on little pillars, held silver serving dishes and trays, and a matching dresser on the opposite side of the room was layered with patterned china. There was an oval-shaped carpet beneath the table, surrounded by polished wooden floorboards and long, dark green velvet curtains hung at the windows. The same day I was able to take a quick peep round the partly open door of the drawing-room and glimpsed a very low settee and comfortable armchairs covered with chintzes, big standard lamps and bowls of flowers on a couple of occasional tables.

In spite of all the elaborate furnishings and affluent atmosphere around the house, I had a strange feeling that somehow the rooms lacked something and realised eventually that there were none of the usual family photographs on view anywhere - not a single bouncing baby, smiling bride and groom, nor pretty child sitting smugly at a piano.

The gardens were mostly lawned, with wide borders of rose trees and variegated laurel bushes and a big vegetable patch behind the orchard - all looked after by an old man who lived near to Highfield Terrace. He used to touch his cap whenever he caught sight of members of the household and I was once highly amused when he gave me a similar salute as I came out of a side door, although he always ignored me completely in our neighbourhood. Apart from at the tea-party I saw the retired major on a few occasions at a distance only, when he just nodded vaguely in my direction. Mrs Pedlow came into the library sometimes while I was waiting for Eve and spoke to me briefly in a stiff and formal way; she looked much more like a well-preserved grandmother than an aunt, and her dignified manner and pearl choker necklaces and earrings reminded me of Queen Mary, to whom I had once waved along with the rest of my class from the pavement in Victoria Road.

One summer, Grammar School staff organised a day trip to London on our behalf. We assembled at Runcorn railway station and, before boarding the train, were each given a paper bag containing two sausage rolls, a small packet of Marie biscuits and an orange - intended as total sustenance for the day. The railway line was littered with empty paper bags and most of the sausage rolls had also been flung out of the windows before the train even reached Crewe. At the age of twelve it was the first time in my life I had travelled further than on a family outing to Rhyl. We were not forced to wear school uniform, and Eve looked a perfect little lady in her fawn covet-coating suit and matching tam-o'-shanter. I was attired in one of Beth's jackets, and the elastic on the Panama hat Mother had rammed over my Eton crop that morning left an angry red mark under my chin.

Sad to relate, my friendship with Eve ended abruptly and totally inexplicably. There was no answer to my pull on the bell-rope one Monday morning and no signs of life whatever around the house. Four bottles of milk stood unheeded on the front steps and the curtains had disappeared from the windows. Neither school staff nor the old gardener had been informed of any impending move, but it was rumoured later that a large van with "High Speed Removals, Essex" painted on its sides had transported all the household belongings to an unknown destination at the weekend. I felt sure that Eve would write to me from her new home to explain everything, but she didn't. The house was put up for sale and as far as I know no-one ever saw or heard from the strange occupants of "Birchwood" again, and their two-year stay in Runcorn and hurried departure from it were cloaked in mystery forever.

Throughout those two years I'd seen little of Dorothy Dawson, but discovered that after a series of elocution lessons she'd begun to speak in an artificially refined way and developed an infuriating habit of pausing before some words (particularly any starting with an aspirate) and then pronouncing them very clearly and correctly. In fact she quite often added aspirates when she shouldn't have done. The pastel-coloured dresses had by then been replaced by fashionable teenage-style garments and although on weekdays she was restricted to school uniform like everyone else, hers came from the illustrious Browns of

Chester. (Apart from a few items passed down by my cousins, Mother bought mine at the local Co-op). She usually joined in with the school's summer camps, but the year after Eve left Runcorn, Mrs Dawson surprisingly invited me to go with them on their annual family week's holiday to Blackpool - with all expenses paid! I was thrilled with the idea, especially as I'd never had a holiday away from home, and my friendship with Dorothy blossomed once more when I accepted the invitation with joyful alacrity.

I didn't really enjoy myself, mainly because (a) my neglect of aspirates was criticised constantly by Dorothy, (b) Mr Dawson (who was diabetic) made my stomach turn over every morning by demonstrating how he injected insulin from a syringe into his arm and (c) to allay my current mild dose of acne, Mrs Dawson forcibly injected Bile Beans into me every night. However, the combination of the Bile Beans and the Blackpool breezes certainly improved my complexion and I returned to Runcorn with the additional satisfaction of having accomplished my very first week's holiday away from home.

Shortly afterwards the Dawsons moved from Churchfield Terrace and bought a much larger house at the other end of the town so that (according to her mother) Dorothy would have better social advantage later on. Mr Dawson had a reasonably good job at the tannery, but in order to help pay off the resultant mortgage, he and his wife had to keep a tight rein on the family budget, even to the extent of making personal sacrifice. Their economies included his taking a frugal couple of bananas for his weekday lunch at the now-distant tannery warehouse, and habitually writing dates on eggs laid by hens in their back garden, so that there could be no danger of Mrs Dawson using them out of turn and thereby risk one going off. They always managed to ensure, however, that their daughter never went short of anything that money could buy.

After learning during the course of the holiday in Blackpool that Dorothy had a number of penfriends, I decided to follow suit. I got a few names and addresses via her contacts and started off enthusiastically by corresponding with Fiona Patterson in Scotland and Ilse Weirmatt in Germany.

To my dismay I soon realised that Fiona possessed more material assets than Dorothy and all my fee-paying acquaintances put together. Her letters came on fancy notepaper, with coloured flowers and animals painted in the corners and on the matching envelopes, and she wrote that she was driven to a private academy each day by the family chauffeur, owned a pony and two dogs and went for weekly lessons in ballet dancing. In a desperate attempt to overcome my consequent sense of inferiority, I invented my own pony called Scramble, two dogs and a cat, and for good measure threw Peter and Paul - a couple of hamsters - into my replies. On paper I elevated myself to a fee-paying scholar at the Grammar School, and admitted ruefully that I, too, had difficulty in mastering pirouettes and pas-de-deux at my (non-existent) dancing lessons. After learning that Fiona was but one of her many Christian names, I explained hurriedly that the Freda with which I had signed my first epistle was actually just a convenient abbreviation of the Frederica Veronica Anastasia with which I'd been christened, and I gradually contributed all sorts of exciting events to my accounts of normally humdrum daily life in Runcorn. Most of them were manufactured from stories in "The Girls' Own Paper" which I sincerely hoped didn't circulate in Scotland!

I had an extremely nasty shock when in a letter from north of the border Fiona informed me suddenly that she and her parents were planning to visit relatives in Liverpool. According to her geography atlas, she wrote, it seemed to be quite near to Runcorn, so wouldn't it be absolutely marvellous if she could come to my home for a wee spell and be introduced to Scramble and company? If her father put her on the train at Liverpool, perhaps I'd meet her at Runcorn station, and we could each wear a flower on our lapels for easy recognition? I struggled desperately to think of a way out of my web of deceit, knowing full well that if she did come to No. 12 it would be very difficult for me to explain the absence of all the imaginary pets and, worse still, to account for the variance between the true characteristics of members of my family and those I had penned so glowingly. After a disturbed night during which every possible solution I thought up seemed to end in a cul-de-sac, recollection of Eve's sudden departure from "Birchwood" sprang to my mind miraculously as soon as I woke up the next morning (as things so often do just at daybreak) and I sent off a hurried note to Fiona to let her know that Dad's tannery (which my previous letters had indicated he actually owned) was transferring at once to the outskirts of Portsmouth and, although devastated at missing the opportunity of meeting up with her, I should regrettably have to postpone further correspondence until we'd settled in our new abode. I received one more letter from her, with "PLEASE FORWARD TO NEW ADDRESS" marked in block capitals below a picture of two little rabbits hopping across the envelope. The inscription must have baffled our regular postman completely, but I never found courage enough to write to Fiona again. I sometimes wonder whether she assumed sadly that we'd all been involved in a tragic accident on our way south in the large Hillman of my earlier fabrication.

Letters between me and the German girl were very boring. Ilse asked for them to be written in English only, so that she could improve her knowledge of the language, but after I had considerately conveyed mundane bits like, "I have a brother and a sister" and, "I go to church on Sundays" once or twice, her equally stilted replies of, "A sister is in my house but not a boy," and, "To church we go too" scarcely caused me to jump for joy, and the novelty of corresponding with her wore off quickly. One afternoon all pupils who had German penfriends were summoned to the headmaster's office at school and warned not to pass on to them any information about ports, cities or communications in our area. At the time the request seemed to be totally incomprehensible, but the advent of the Second World War was to clarify it to some extent a few years later. I reckon, however, that Hitler gained little if correspondence between other British and German youngsters was as unfruitful as mine to Ilse must have been proved to be. When I returned to the classroom and told the English mistress of the outcome of the Head's unexpected summons, she nodded slowly, "Ah... A chiel's amang ye takin' notes, as Robbie Burns said," she murmured - determined as always to make the most of any opportunity to instil into us an item from her vast treasury of literary quotations.

# Chapter 12

When Beth stopped taking music lessons and practising scales on the piano in the parlour at No. 12 because her nervous spasms seemed to be multiplying as a result, I felt attracted to the pianoforte aspect myself and tried to persuade Mother to send me for some lessons from Beth's former tutor. She obviously wasn't to be swayed easily, despite the fact that for a while I strove to curry favour by showing a sudden willingness to run errands and help with the washing-up, and even volunteered to carry the wireless battery to the shop for its periodic recharge (reminding her that in so doing I ran the risk of getting my hands burned by the acid slopping out at the top). Unhappily all my conniving fell on stony ground.

"We can't afford it and you'd never have enough patience to practise scales, anyway," Mother told me.

"Yes, I should!" I insisted. "I'd do them for at least an hour every night!"

"If you did that you'd never get through your homework," Grandma instantly chipped in. "And look what doing them every night's done to Beth!" As usual, her opinion settled the matter once and for all.

In exasperation, I decided to tutor myself. I found that by following the top lines of notes shown in music scores I was able to pick out tunes quite easily with my right hand, especially after I'd pencilled circles round the bits for which my ears suggested I should depress black keys. Beth had apparently progressed from playing little ditties like "The Lonely Shepherd Boy" and "Down There in the Valley" to compositions by

*Solo Effort.*

Beethoven, Schubert and Strauss, and there were also four volumes of Gilbert and Sullivan operettas (obtained at a reduced price after she'd cut out six coupons from the "News Chronicle") tucked away in the piano stool. However, I decided to limit my efforts to pieces from "The Complete Methodist Hymn Book" (because I knew most of the tunes in that anyway) and "Songs for the Fireside", containing items such as "Genevieve" and "Rocked in the Cradle of the Deep", which at one time had lightened the boredom of long Victorian evenings and were vaguely familiar to me from Mother's warblings around the house. My left hand merely tum-tummed on white keys at the bottom end of the piano, but I was well satisfied with the general outcome and often used to open the parlour window wide (particularly just after the tannery hooter had signalled the end of a day's work there), so that passers-by could be made fully aware of my imagined expertise.

Apart from at Christmas, parlours in most homes in our neighbourhood were used almost solely for any necessary lying-in-state of a deceased member of the household. The family at No. 12 rarely ventured into ours and in time I began to look upon it as a private haven of retreat. During the few months before my matriculation exams I was allowed the luxury of a one-bar electric fire in the hearth so that I could do homework undisturbed.

In addition to the piano there was a big mahogany cabinet which housed Dad's RAOB regalia and cheap little souvenirs inscribed "A Present from Llandudno", "Blackpool Tower" and so on, which we'd brought back from our day trips to the seaside. A plush velvet three-piece suite, bookcase and a small table pushed against the bay window were somehow squashed into the rest of the room. The fireplace was black marble, with carved pillars on each side and a big onyx clock (which never worked) on the mantelshelf. Large gilt-framed paintings on the wall portrayed "A Fallen Idol", "The Stag at Bay" and "The Bounty" (one of W and H Cooper's boats which sank in the River Mersey with a set of Uncle Peter's false teeth on board). I used to think naively that the stricken man in "The Fallen Idol" was for some ill-mannered reason refusing to help the tearful woman to her feet after a fall, and the mournful eyes of "The Stag at Bay" reminded me of Jesus on the wall at Sunday School. Later on the pictures were replaced by "The Boyhood of Raleigh", "When did you last see your father?" and "The Laughing Cavalier", all of which Dad procured by saving up hundreds of coupons from Wills' Capstan Cigarette packets.

I'm afraid my homework was pushed aside occasionally when I was tempted to browse through some of the volumes on the bookshelves. Most of the Webster children's Sunday School prizes were still intact, also Beth's encyclopedias, which I could now reach fairly easily without the help of a chair, and I was especially intrigued by "The Home Doctor" - although I soon found that, like the encyclopedias, each item in it referred you to other parts for further enlightenment. At least everything was included in one volume, but I became quite worried once when I started to search for a cure for my slight cold and after thumbing through a number of pages appeared to justify immediate admission into a TB sanatorium!

In intervening years improvements had been carried out in the living quarters at No. 12. The big black grate and oven had been replaced by a tiled fireplace - with a consequent increase of a shilling on the weekly rental paid to the tannery (and the additional cost of several packets of Keating's powder needed to kill off a swarm of cockroaches which must previously have kept comfortably warm behind the oven). As electricity had by then been introduced into the terrace we acquired a modern cooker, and when the old flat irons were substituted by an electric one, Mother was able to dispense with the beeswax altogether.

At that time the Methodist Circuit in Runcorn used to organise annual Eisteddfods in one or other of the Sunday School halls; scholars were invited to demonstrate their vocal and literary talents, and prizes were awarded for the most meritorious entries. One young girl from our church won the singing competition for three years running, although her song choices of "Danny Boy", "One alone to be my own" and "Blue heavens and you and I" seemed rather inappropriate for someone who had scarcely reached her teens. I once won a prize in the Art section for my sketch of a window in the ruins of Halton Castle and another the following year for an essay describing "An imaginary trip in an aeroplane." The latter wasn't quite so imaginative as it was supposed to be, because one of the heroines in "The Girls' Own Paper" had most obligingly crossed the English Channel by air in a fairly recent issue.

That literary success encouraged me to enter a competition advertised in the "Liverpool Weekly Post" for the best article entitled "Why I am against smoking." It was obviously intended to attract contributions from adults but, ever resourceful, I penned a variety of comments on the subject in Mother's name and sent them off without her knowledge. The following week she was amazed to see, "Mrs Elizabeth Bray's prize winning entry" printed in the paper. Fortunately she agreed with what I'd written and passed on her award of five pounds.

Dissatisfied with my almost non-existent social life, I joined the Girl Guides. There were three contingents of the movement in the town; I was attached to the 1st Runcorn troop and designated to the Robin Patrol. Each of the four patrols were named after birds and had a patrol leader and a second-in-command. Our captain was Miss Boston, and our headquarters were in a big wooden hut specially constructed at her home, "The Grange" (which in time was to become the administrative centre for the local council). The extensive grounds there provided ample opportunities for nature trails and camp fires, and before long I boasted an assortment of badges on the sleeve of my Guide tunic to confirm my dexterity in various pursuits. They did not, of course, include any for needlecraft, cookery or housewifery. Once the whole troop went to sing carols at Dutton Workhouse, the institution on the outskirts of the town where destitutes had once been sent to live out their lives. Part of it was being used currently as a geriatric hospital, but it still housed several homeless people.

The building was of very dark brick, with immense matching chimneys, and was surrounded by a high wall. The dreary accommodation inside the section we visited seemed to consist mainly of a big eating room and a number of dormitories in which narrow iron beds (some with adjustable side rails) were pushed closely together. The elderly inmates were reasonably clean, but their clothes looked as if they might have been handed down through several decades. Because they spent all their time indoors, their faces were sallow and also wrinkled by age. In fact, their generally unkempt appearance, wistful expressions and the obvious stigma connected with their surroundings took most of the joy out of our carolling. Miss Boston was so distressed by the prevailing circumstances that she arranged for our troop to give a concert in the Baths Hall just before the next Christmas, and we bought seasonal gifts for inmates of the workhouse out of the proceeds.

My interest in the Girl Guides evaporated rather quickly when most of them around my age were entering the senior branch of the movement, known as Rangers, and I decided I'd rather join in with the young people's ballroom dancing at evening sessions in a couple of public halls. For a fee of one shilling you first watched the teachers demonstrating the various steps and then practised them with a partner, to the accompaniment of either a piano or a wind-up gramophone. At one of the halls you also got a cup of tea and a biscuit halfway through the proceedings.

Whenever possible I went along to the Wednesday evening gatherings at the Guild Hall, and found that my old friend Maureen attended them regularly. By then she'd already left school and was working alongside her Aunt Elsie in Glover's laundry. For the dancing sessions she wore tight skirts of shiny black material and gaudy tops festooned with strings of beads across the cleavage of her bosom, and tottered around in extremely high-heeled tarnished slippers. Her peroxided and frizzed-up hair was spattered with grips ornamented with little diamante stars, and her rouged cheeks jutted out sharply from a thick layer of chalk-white face powder. Beside her I felt uncomfortably childish and drab, because what few clothes I possessed in addition to my school uniform were suitable primarily for churchgoing, and none of them could by any stretch of the imagination be termed glamorous. My make-up was limited to a touch of Tokalon Vanishing Cream (reputed to be used by famous film stars like Jean Harlow and Loretta Young) and a smear of Grandma's foot-soothing vaseline to make my eyelashes look longer. I did manage to overcome my dress predicament sometimes by delving (without permission) into Beth's wardrobe. Her things weren't really what anyone would class as fashionable but at least they were an improvement on my short-sleeved belted prints and fitted me reasonably well.

My enjoyment of those evenings, however, was marred a bit by scornful scrutiny from Maureen and her new pals.

"Have you got a boyfriend yet?" she queried one night as she peered critically at our joint reflection in the cracked wall mirror at the Guild Hall. The acquisition of friends of the opposite sex was clearly of paramount importance to her, and when I admitted shame-facedly that I hadn't she turned to eye me quickly from head to toe.

"Try getting your hair permed now that it's grown properly," she suggested. "It might make a difference and it only costs five bob at Audrey's in Halton Road. She does Eugenes and Wellas and knocks sixpence off if you go on a Monday. Shall I ask her if she can fit you in next week?" When I explained dolefully that I should need to save up my pocket money for at least a month before I'd be able to afford a perm even at the reduced cost, Maureen shrugged her shoulders and said that in her opinion I should leave school without further ado, and considerately offered to help me get a job in the laundry.

The dancing lessons took place in the largest room in the hall and collapsible chairs were set out for the occupation of girls on one side and boys on the other. We were supervised by a middle-aged couple from Liverpool who called themselves Adrian and Belle (though rumour had it that their real names were Arthur and Beattie), who had an abundance of gold and silver medals pinned to their chests. Their nephew, a spotty-faced lad with big ears, used to sprinkle boracic powder on the floor before we started and he also wound up the gramophone. We progressed from the waltz and quickstep to a Doris Waltz, Yearning Saunter, Tango and Foxtrot, and occasionally attempted the more boisterous Military Two-Step and Gay Gordons. At Adrian's command of, "Take your partners for..." there was always an initial scurry of boys dashing across to claim girls of their choice, but the remainder had to be more or less forced to their feet by Belle. As girls were usually in the majority, some were left to pair off together. The proceedings ended with a last waltz under dimmed lighting, and I noticed that Maureen and her friends drifted off into the darkness afterwards with the boys who'd picked them up for that.

The spotty lad also organised weekly raffles to boost takings, and one night the prize was astonishingly a ticket for a free flight in an aeroplane from a field in the neighbourhood at which short hops were being put on offer at five shillings a time for three consecutive Saturday afternoons to give local people a chance to enjoy what was then a fascinating new pastime. My partner drew out the winning ticket but confessed he would be too scared to make the flight himself, and to my great delight passed it on to me.

I presented myself at the field the very next Saturday afternoon, in case the arrangements were later abandoned for bad weather or any other reason. The two planes in use were quite small and waddled rather alarmingly as they rose into the sky, but I was overjoyed to be strapped into one of them and circle above Runcorn and Widnes for my allotted ten minutes. The River Mersey, Manchester Ship and Bridgewater Canals and bridges over them were plainly visible, and I convinced myself that the small smudge in a garden behind Highfield Terrace would be Dad planting potato sets. I was disappointed that we didn't loop-the-loop but apparently that wasn't included in my free trip and would have cost an extra seven shillings and sixpence.

I must admit that although for the most part my adolescence was spent in making unenthusiastic academic progress at the Grammar School, it did have a few lighter moments.

# Chapter 13

My last year at the Grammar School flew by and when I was sixteen I sat the Joint Matriculation Board examinations, which for most fifth-formers in Cheshire marked the end of their education.

The principles on which the Board based its awards were rather complicated, and effectively demanded higher standards than assessment of the total number of successes in a variety of subjects (including those as easily digested as Home Economics and Religious Knowledge) which was introduced as the yardstick for measuring pupils' academic achievement later on. The Matriculation Board acting jointly for the universities of Manchester, Liverpool, Leeds, Sheffield and Birmingham stipulated that candidates had to get minimum "passes" in English Language, English Literature and Mathematics and additionally in (a) at least one Science subject, (b) at least one foreign language and (c) Art, History or Geography. If those essentials were satisfied, a School Certificate was awarded to the candidate. Marks much higher than "pass" level earned "credit" or "distinction" ratings and credits and/or distinctions in five or more subjects within the set groupings gained a Matriculation standard award.

In the 1930's it was customary for boys and girls with good results and who were keen to be admitted to a university or the teaching profession to continue in a sixth form at school for two more years, with a view to acquiring the Higher or Subsidiary School Certificate essential for such further progress. It was unusual for girls in particular to aim at specialised careers because they offered guaranteed prospects to those with exceptional ability only and involved long years of training which few parents could afford to support. The sixth form at the Runcorn Grammar School consisted generally of one or two boys hoping for university scholarships, and a handful of girls waiting to equip themselves later on as teachers. They occupied a single classroom and were given individual tuition by staff.

Of those who left at the end of their year in the fifth form, the majority of girls from the A stream usually opted for some form of clerical work. A few went on to private commercial colleges for secretarial training, although at sixteen plus they were at a disadvantage in competing for jobs alongside pupils from the Secondary Schools (who were able to leave when they were fourteen after doing typewriting within the normal curriculum there). Child care and nursing seemed to appeal only to the daughters of doctors and clergymen. Girls from the B form took routine clerical jobs (Dorothy was hoping to become a clerk/telephonist) or went into factories or shops, where vacancies were numerous but the pay was poor. Boys fared little better concerning availability of choice in the job market, excepting that in addition to being offered vacancies in offices and banks, etc, they also stood a fair chance of getting work of a technical nature in research laboratories at big chemical complexes in our area (especially if their fathers worked there already).

Matriculation results were published halfway through the summer holidays, and school staff appeared to presume that anyone who gained necessary qualifications and wished to go into the sixth form would return the following September without special prior instruction of any kind. The words of the hymn we always sang on the last day of final terms - "Let thy Father-hand be shielding all who here shall meet no more" -

were apparently expected to provide succour enough for the remainder.

My scholarship was due to terminate at the end of the summer term in which I had taken the matriculation exam, and I'd decided some time earlier that I should like to train for a job in teaching. I knew that County Scholarship holders could extend their free education, so I hoped for similar concession from the Highfield Tanning Company. Unfortunately Dad was totally opposed to the idea, and refused to make any approach to the firm on my behalf - not even by means of a "Craving your kind indulgence" letter - and I was left to pursue whatever I thought to be the best line of action myself.

I had no knowledge of correct protocol in such matters whatever, but I looked up (in the directory in the telephone kiosk in Halton Road) the address of one of the directors of the firm. I dressed up in my best clothes one evening and walked the two miles to his house. On the way I tried to work out what I would say when I got there, and decided that for a start it might be diplomatic to thank him (albeit belatedly) for the one pound Savings Bank deposit the company had invested for me at birth - which it did for each child of its employees. By the time I'd made up a suitable little speech I'd arrived at his house. It was quite an impressive place with a tree-lined drive and a couple of big stone steps at the front, and the white-capped maid who answered my ring at the door reminded me of my calls at "Birchwood".

Once inside the hall (which looked about half the size of the Guild Hall dance floor) I felt as if I'd dipped one foot into icy water and was no longer keen to take the necessary plunge. I must have somehow managed to convey the reason for my unexpected visit to the maid, however, because she went up the wide staircase and a few moments later her employer appeared, attired in a black dinner suit and struggling to get a bow-tie into position as he hurried down the stairs. His damp hair gave the impression that he'd recently come out of the bath, and I realised with dismay that I might have timed my visit inopportunely.

Although I'd often seen him passing Highfield Terrace in his car on his way to the works, I guessed that he was unlikely to recognise me. I shuffled my feet and cleared my throat nervously.

"Good evening," I started off primly, in a voice which didn't sound at all like my own. "I'm Freda Bray and I won the tannery scholarship a few years ago."

"Oh, yes?" he queried politely, still tugging at the tie and looking as if his thoughts were really elsewhere.

The speech I'd thought up on the way to his house had vanished into thin air, and for a second I wished there was a nearby hole into which I could crawl. Then I remembered my desperate need for his assistance.

"Well... my exam results are good and I'm hoping the firm will pay for me to stay on at school for another two years so that I can go in for teaching," I gabbled on, adding just in time "... please."

He abandoned the tie and looked at me as if he'd suddenly come down to earth. "No - I'm afraid not," he replied at once. "Your scholarship expired last month, and has already been re-allocated. Extension isn't often given. I'm sorry to disappoint you, but we must stick to our present company rules. As a matter of fact, I was told the name of the successful candidate for the next place this morning. Will you excuse me now? I'm just dressing for dinner and in a bit of a hurry..." With that he turned and went back up the stairs and the maid re-appeared from nowhere to show me out.

Years later I appreciated that a variety of circumstances could have affected the situation and in accordance with the firm's current policy his refusal was probably quite justified, but just then I felt it was grossly unfair, and rage bubbled inside me. Obviously I was to be denied the premise of the final words of the school's end-of-term hymn - "... Those returning make more faithful than before" - and I sobbed and snuffled all the way home.

I received no sympathy back at No. 12.

"Far better to get a job straight away than waste another two years at school and goodness knows how many more at a teachers' training college after that!" was the general feeling there, and Grandma added unsurprisingly, "I did warn you about the monkey, didn't I?"

Beth's offer to try to get me fixed up in the office where she worked met with approval all round, although Uncle Peter's caustic reminder that if Dad hadn't been so eager to put a feather in his own cap I might now, like some of my friends, be able to continue studies at the expense of the County Council, naturally fired off another sulk. Mother and Dad had footed the cost of Beth's short secretarial course at a commercial college, and already arranged for Fred to be bound for seven years as apprentice wheelwright with the Manchester Ship Canal Company as soon as he finished at Balfour Road Boys' School, but during the three-day period of communal silence following Peter's untimely remark I didn't dare suggest that they might offer to pay my school fees, which would have totalled £18 for the two years plus the cost of textbooks.

Youth Employment and Career Advice schemes were unheard of, and at that time Labour Exchanges provided little assistance to school leavers apart from recording a few personal details in readiness for any sudden rush of vacancies. Beth was told that there were no current jobs for which I might be considered suitable in her office in Widnes, so for a few weeks

117

I drifted like flotsam, filling in the time reading books from the library and scanning local newspapers for job openings.

One day I noticed an advertisement in a national paper concerning entry into the Civil Service via open competition, and wrote off for further details. To my surprise the Commission gave no credit at all for previous academic achievement; candidates were apparently required to pass special written examinations held in various British cities, and if successful were liable to be assigned to posts in Government departments in any part of the country. Three of the cities named were within daily travelling distance of Runcorn. After a lot of form-filling I sat the Open Clerical Class Examination (the standard of which was roughly equivalent to Matriculation Board papers) in Chester in November that year.

I had to wait until the following March for the results, so I started to look around for some sort of employment to occupy me temporarily in the interim period - or permanently if I didn't pass the exam. I soon discovered that vacancies for inexperienced clerical workers were scarce and that quite often firms advertised posts which they'd already decided to fill by the promotion of current staff and their newspaper insertions were mere formalities.

In response to one of my applications for accounts work I was invited to go for interview at the Electricity Board's office in Runcorn. After deciding reluctantly that Beth's wardrobe held nothing really suitable for the occasion, I took my only mustard-checked suit along to the cleaners and arranged for it to be dyed brown, in belief that a sombre colour would produce a better image of me as a competent clerk. Mother, who was understandably fed up with seeing me lazing around at home, paid for me to get my hair shampooed and set, and on the morning of the interview inspected my finger nails critically, commenting that would-be employers always notice such things.

I set off hopefully, but felt somewhat deflated when a receptionist at the office told me that I was the last of twelve applicants chosen to be interviewed for the vacancy. The girl ahead of me was wearing a very plain navy blue pinstripe suit and a Robin Hood style hat with a feather at the side. While we were waiting she ignored me completely, but I put that down to nervousness, because she kept clutching her handbag in first one hand and then the other and, just as her name was called, she dropped it altogether and the contents spilled out across the floor. By the time she'd collected all the bits and pieces and rammed them into her bag her cheeks were scarlet and the feather was distinctly askew. She was in and out of the inner sanctum in three minutes flat.

My appointment had been timed for 10 o'clock; the abrupt departure of the girl in front of me brought it forward by about fifteen minutes, but it still didn't end until just before 12 o'clock. The reason for its unusual longevity was due to the fact that I'd mentioned on my application form that I was a Sunday School teacher: apparently my interviewer (a suave and rather pompous individual who peered at me appraisingly over the top of gold-rimmed spectacles) belonged to a peculiar religious sect, and we somehow became involved in prolonged discussion on the differences between Methodist-based beliefs and his own. He didn't succeed in converting me but the best part of two hours went by in heated argument over Biblical prophecies concerning the afterlife. He showed no interest at all in my Matriculation Board's result card and, after a surprised glance at his watch, eventually dismissed me with the perfunctory, "We'll let you know" with which I was unfortunately becoming only too familiar. The next day I received a brief note telling me that the vacancy was to be filled by someone else. As the wages were a scant ten shillings a week and the receptionist had chanced to mention that the duties would include making tea twice a day for the gentleman who was doing the interviewing, I wasn't particularly sorry that I hadn't been successful.

In the end I did manage to get a job at a Mail Order Store office in Liverpool, which seemed to advertise a stream of vacancies regularly in the "Liverpool Echo". My written application was accepted there instantly and I was given a starting date without interview.

I worked from 8 am to 5 pm on weekdays and up to noon on Saturdays, and had to leave home at 6.30 in the morning in order to catch the 7 o'clock train to Lime Street. Oftener than not I ran most of the distance to Runcorn railway station along the canal towpath and sometimes gobbled down a bacon or fried egg sandwich on the way. The train used to stop at all other stations en route, and I was usually left with little more than ten minutes in which to dash across slippery tram-lines and through the almost-deserted Liverpool streets and clock-in at the office for 8 o'clock. I soon found out that a few other girls from Runcorn worked there too and travelled by the same train, and one morning when it was exceptionally late the one with the longest legs volunteered to run ahead and stamp our time-cards to avoid late attendances being recorded against us (which would have resulted in the stoppage of half an hour's pay). The rest of us still trotted along as fast as we could, but when we arrived breathless at the entrance to the building several minutes later, our forerunner was standing outside in tears - a supervisor had caught her in the act and sacked her on the spot.

My wages were seventeen shillings a week, out of which I paid five shillings a week for rail fares. The job consisted solely of counting and sorting customers' mailed orders and sticking them on to labelled hooks ready for transfer to various parts of the warehouse. It was tediously repetitive, and although girls working alongside me were full of typically good-natured

Liverpudlian humour we had little in common, because their chatter seemed to centre on the boyfriends who absorbed their interest outside working hours and I had nothing at all to subscribe in that respect.

However, my boredom was eased slightly when I was invited to play for the firm's hockey team on Saturday afternoons. To my delight I was placed in the centre-forward position I'd coveted at school; most of our matches were against opponents from various other business concerns in the district, at sportsgrounds on the outskirts of the city.

One week we were scheduled to go to Bryant and Mays' Matchworks at Garston, and as soon as the finishing bell rang at noon I hurried along to eat a snack lunch with the rest of our team before setting off by bus. I was intercepted by one of my supervisors, who unexpectedly ordered me to go up to the Personnel Office. The clerk there had a round, flabby face and a shiny balding head, and I wasn't sure whether the vague wave of his hand as I went into the room was intended to smooth his thinning hair or indicate that I should sit down. I remained standing and he came straight to the point.

"I understand you're waiting for results of a Civil Service exam, Miss Bray?" Although I was surprised that he was aware of the fact, I merely thought that it was nice of him to be taking an interest in my doings.

"Yes," I answered promptly, "but they're not due until the end of this month at the earliest."

"And if you're successful... what do you plan to do then?" he asked.

"Oh - I'll have to go wherever I'm sent," I informed him blithely. "Postings can be to anywhere in the country, but on the other hand I might be lucky enough to get one in Chester or Liverpool." The man frowned, opened a drawer in the desk in front of him and held out a sealed wage-packet.

"In that case you may as well terminate your services with our firm today," he announced. "The seventeen shillings in this envelope are in lieu of a week's notice and I'll post your stamped insurance card on to you next Monday."

"But - I'm not at all sure I'll pass the exam," I stammered, ignoring his outstretched hand. "There were hundreds of other entrants all over the country."

"Well, that's your own concern," he replied flatly. "I'm afraid we can't waste time here training staff who are just hangers-on." I pocketed the wage envelope and walked out of the room without further comment. The captain of the hockey team was the only person in the office to whom I'd mentioned the Civil Service exam, and I had a shrewd idea that it was she who'd thrown a spiteful spanner into the works because our supervisor had recently complimented me on the remarkable speed at which I was getting orders on to the hooks. With a mental two-fingered gesture to both her and the firm I decided that they could also forego my services in the realm of sport, and caught the next train back to Runcorn.

"What a pity!" Mother sighed when I arrived home with my hockey stick much earlier than expected and told her that because of a drop in orders the store had been compelled to reduce its staff. Of course Grandma's monkey slid down the stick, and she tacked on, "You'd better keep away from offices from now on, because they're always throwing out people just when it suits them!" With difficulty I bit back an urge to question her personal experience in such matters, and accepted miserably that I should have to go job hunting again as soon as possible.

The following week Mother spotted a large advertisement in the "Liverpool Echo".

"Oh, look!," she pointed out eagerly, "they need clerks in the mail order place! Their orders must have picked up again!

You'd better write in straight away!" I should have found it difficult to explain my way out of that dilemma, and was considerably relieved when the very next day I heard that I'd passed the Civil Service exam.

Results were given on lists showing candidates' marks at each examination centre, with a line drawn below an initial block of the names of those to be offered immediate vacancies. To my great satisfaction I saw that my name was well above the line, and an accompanying letter assured me of an early posting as a clerical officer in Chester at a salary of £93 a year.

The news came by first post on Good Friday, and in the afternoon I went for a celebratory five-mile walk in swirling flurries of snow, feeling extremely pleased with myself and convinced that the bad luck which seemed to have dogged my progress in one way or another for so long had at last run out. It was as if someone had appeared just as I was facing a firing-squad and shouted, "Hold it! She's reprieved!" A month later, after a satisfactory medical examination by a designated consultant in Manchester (for a fee of ten shillings and at which I recall with amusement the only receptacle he was able to present for the urine test was an outsized Victorian plant pot), I received welcome instructions to start work at the Telephone Manager's Office in St John Street in Chester on 6th May.

Mother immediately bought me a new outfit, including a grey velour hat which she insisted was proper for anyone entering His Majesty's Service - and which I wore once only - and Dad unexpectedly gave me six shillings to pay for my first weekly rail contract.

"Where's the monkey now?" I taunted Grandma gleefully. "Right at the top of its stick?"

She merely gave a derisive snort, and repeated Uncle Peter's old adage.

"Like Mr Asquith said - let's wait and see!"

# Chapter 14

Runcorn changed in many ways during my teens.

Imperial Chemical Industries took over most of the existing chemical works and in addition opened up larger factories; the tanneries expanded, and the canals and docks were busier than ever. As a result of the industrial progress, wages improved and most workers were able to maintain a good standard of living throughout the year and also take their families for regular summer holidays.

There was a lot of building activity. Large residential estates were put up in three separate districts, and new developments of privately-owned houses appeared all over the place. The latter were mainly semi-detached, standing in short roads or cul-de-sacs, and Baby Austins and motorcycles with sidecars parked outside them indicated that their owners still had cash to spare after the mortgage had been paid. The growing number of old push-bikes and prams discarded into the Bridgewater Canal caused Uncle Peter to comment sarcastically that nowadays everybody seemed to have far too much money to throw around. Inhabitants of older houses in the town started to busy themselves with home improvements on a do-it-yourself basis, and a couple of plumbers from the tannery came along to turn third bedrooms into bathrooms for the benefit of some of the residents in Highfield Terrace.

Unfortunately accommodation problems at No. 12 prevented us from having similar amenity. Admittedly baths were still a problem for us, but Aunt Emma and her family had moved into a small semi-detached house (in a cul-de-sac named

Marina Grove after the new Duchess of Kent) which had a tiny bathroom, and kindly invited Beth and me to go there every Sunday morning for thorough cleansing. In winter, Beth was apt to have one of her nervous spasms afterwards; we provided our own soap and towels and were permitted only one helping of hot water, so we took turns for the first dip. When mine was second, I cheated by topping up very quietly, drop by drop. Everyone else at home still used the bath under the hearthrug in the living-room; Grandma's immersions (with Mother's assistance) were infrequent, but she soaked her feet regularly in an enamel bowl full of hot water in front of the fire and then anointed them with vaseline and boracic powder.

For the first time in my life I started to pay really serious attention to my appearance. In most romantic books and films adolescence is ascribed as the point at which braces on teeth, wiry pigtails and freckles disappear magically and a startling beauty emerges from the chrysalis. I regretted that in my own case there had apparently been no such lightening transformation - although I admit that I hadn't been handicapped by any of the disadvantages mentioned. However, I was convinced that my looks could be improved by a permanent wave, as suggested by Maureen, and as soon as I received my first month's pay from the Civil Service I set aside five shillings for that very purpose.

I didn't go to the Audrey of my old pal's choice, but made a Saturday afternoon appointment at a salon in Higher Runcorn which looked much more impressive than the dingy little shop in Halton Road. I went in rather tentatively, hung up my coat alongside the picture of a model displaying a glamorous hair-do which I hoped sincerely mine would resemble at the end of the afternoon, and was told to sit down and look at a magazine until one of the assistants could deal with me. After a while one beckoned me over to a chair in front of a wash-bowl and enveloped me with a huge rubber cape. I surrendered myself dubiously to the mercy of her vicious-looking scissors and nervously watched hunks of my hair falling to the floor. Fortunately there seemed to be enough left for the remainder to be split up and wound tightly round heavy metal rollers before she stuffed my ears with cotton wool and sponged my head all over with a smelly solution which dripped down on to my forehead and made my eyes smart. The rollers were then connected via thick corded tubes to a cowl-like device hanging from the ceiling, and by the time all the bits and pieces were in place I felt as if I had a ton weight on top of my head. The assistant unplugged my ears, pressed an electric switch somewhere and handed me another magazine to read.

I had to sit in that uncomfortable position on a straight-backed, rush-bottomed chair for well over an hour. In fact, the whole process took almost four hours, but in those days perms were more or less guaranteed to last for a minimum of twelve months. After a couple of experimental unwindings I was finally assessed as "cooked enough"; the tubes were disconnected and the rollers tossed into a bowl of soapy water.

I was horrified by the frizzy mass which emerged from the operation - nothing at all like the sleek, softly-curled outcome pictured on the wall.

"Don't worry love," the assistant comforted as she tugged through it mercilessly with a comb, "it's just nice and tight and it'll get softer every time you come in for a shampoo and set." Knowing full well that my finances couldn't possibly be stretched enough for regular visits to the salon, her assurance gave me little consolation.

Once outside the shop I silently bemoaned the fact that I had no headscarf with which to cover the disastrous consequence, and scurried home through unfamiliar back-streets to avoid bumping into any acquaintances. I anticipated that Grandma's monkey would be on the move yet again, but was unprepared for the vehement wrath she poured on me when I got home.

"What a sight you look - just like a golliwog who couldn't leave things the way the good Lord made them!" she accused. "I've never seen hard-earned money wasted so in the whole of my life! I suppose you'll be plastering your face with all that artificial muck next, like those trashy women who tramp around the streets in Liverpool?" She rounded off the attack with her usual derogatory comments on the rising generation, and I took myself out of range quickly.

After a while my pay packet enabled me to go for regular hair-do's and also stock up on decent clothes, especially as, under Civil Service rules, I could look forward to annual salary increments until I was twenty five, and get an additional rise if I were lucky enough to be promoted to a higher grade post. Senior posts in the office were filled by men only, and there were no married women at all on the staff; most of my colleagues were under thirty and quite a few around my own age. We worked from 9 am to 5 pm on weekdays and to 12.30 on Saturdays. I travelled by train from Runcorn to Chester and back daily (glad that my morning trip started a whole hour later than the previous one to Liverpool).

I became particularly pally with Edith Carter, one of my fellow clerical officers who lived in Chester and had passed the same entrance exam as me. She persuaded me to enrol with the Chester branch of the Youth Hostel Association to which she belonged, and sometimes the two of us joined in with their weekend rambles.

By providing cheap overnight short-term accommodation in various localities the association made it easy for youngsters to wander around the countryside on foot or bicycles. Mass accusations against private landowners in the 1930's brought about the re-opening of several neglected footpaths and byways, and resulted in more areas being made accessible to hostellers. Membership was worldwide and it was rumoured that young German spies came to England just before the Second World War and used their YHA affiliation as a means of obtaining undercover information from British counterparts.

The hostels differed vastly from place to place. Usually within reach of good walking and cycling districts, some were mere shacks or tumbled-down farmhouses on lonely fellsides, and others lovely mansions like Hartington and Ilam Halls in Derbyshire, and Troutbeck House in the Lake District. A three-storey terraced house in Chester and "Fox Howl" in Delamere Forest were especially handy for members roaming around Cheshire. Those in unfrequented spots, however, were generally the most popular, although they were not always kept open during winter months and a few were recommended for the use of experienced climbers only.

The charge for a night's lodging at a hostel then was one shilling. Cooking facilities were laid on in reasonably well-equipped kitchens and, where there was a resident warden, ready-cooked meals of ham, eggs and beans, etc were available at breakfast and supper times at a cost of a further one shilling and threepence each. Sleeping quarters were in rooms containing bunk beds (but no other furniture) and at some hostels calico sleeping bags were hired out, although the majority of hikers and cyclists carried their own around in rucksacks, together with a personal supply of tin plates, cups and cutlery. Curtains at windows and carpets on floors were rare, but no extra charge was made for the use of pillows or khaki-coloured bed blankets belonging to the association. There were fixed times for "lights out" (which might vary from hostel to hostel), and also for morning departures.

Some buildings had very antiquated outside toilet and washing facilities, but others were equipped with bathrooms

*"Fox Howl" Youth Hostel, Delamere Forest.*

where aching limbs could be eased in piping-hot water for a limited period and a fee of sixpence, and one or two of the "family" establishments had laundry rooms. In the evenings it was customary for everyone to join together in the common-room for sing-songs, and quite often those over eighteen went round to the local pub for a couple of shandies.

During the winter local branches of the association arranged short walks if no weekend stay was planned, and sometimes also held social evenings and dances, with a view to keeping members in touch with each other. A big Saturday afternoon get-together of all Merseyside members, followed by an evening dance, took place annually around Christmas time in St George's Hall in Liverpool.

Edith and I had several outings in Cheshire, Derbyshire, Yorkshire and Wales with other members of our group - a particularly memorable one being when in attempting with my usual ham-fistedness to light a paraffin stove in readiness for cooking an evening meal I nearly set fire to the hostel at Maeshafn in North Wales. As punishment the warden made me clean all five of his stoves before moving on the next morning, while the rest of the party sat on the wall waiting impatiently to set off for our proposed trek up Moel Fammau.

The following summer Edith and I decided to spread our wings by hostelling for ten days in the Lake District, and made advance bookings in good time at the YHA office in Liverpool. After finishing work on the first Saturday we had a quick lunch at her home and then cycled to the hostel in Longridge, near Preston. Our bikes were the old-fashioned "sit-up-and-beg" type, and the going was hard. Rucksacks strapped to our backs were laden to capacity, and by the time we reached our destination we resembled two weary old women humping the fuel home.

The next day we went up to Troutbeck and on the Monday pedalled on to Long Sleddale, where we'd booked in for the remainder of our holiday and planned to do some rock climbing. On Tuesday morning we awoke to a deluge of rain which didn't cease until the following Sunday night. The narrow valley in which the hostel stood was flooded to a depth of twelve inches and sandbags had to be stacked around the doors to keep out the water. The resident warden and his wife managed to supply us with meals and, as they had at one time been British table-tennis champions, tried to while away the boredom of our isolation by giving repeated demonstrations of their skill. Just as Dad's mania for brass bands had turned me against them for evermore, the endless tip-tapping across the table killed any interest I might have had in the game.

The otherwise disappointing holiday did, however, have compensation for me in the form of Ian Bellingham, a fellow marooned-hosteller. We chatted together a lot while the others were engrossed in the table-tennis sessions, and seemed to have a great many similar likes and dislikes. In fact, I thought he was very nice indeed. He was a lieutenant in the regular Army Intelligence Corps at Chester Castle, but his home was in Truro. It seemed strange that we'd first met so far from the city in which we were both just then spending most of our time.

On the last day at Long Sleddale the sky cleared and we were able to see the surrounding rocky tops which had been shrouded in mist for the past six days. Everyone was keen to get out into the fresh air after the long sojourn indoors, and after discussion over suitable routes we split up into three groups. I was pleased to see that Ian had tagged onto ours and he stayed glued to my side all day.

On Tuesday morning Edith and I started off early in an ambitious attempt to complete our return journey in one go, but when we reached Wigan we were so exhausted that we spent the night in a cheap boarding-house there and did the final lap next day. Ian had booked to stay on at Long Sleddale for another three days, but before I left for home he asked me to meet him again the following week in Chester.

# Chapter 15

Ian was of average height and good-looking in a rugged sort of way. He had dark eyes and thick black hair which curled slightly at the ends.

My own looks and temperament had improved quite a lot by then; after two salary increases (one on my birthday and one resulting from a long-overdue Treasury review of civil servants' pay) I'd managed to accumulate an assortment of quite fashionable clothes, and found it much easier to mix with people once I'd shrugged off the inferiority complex. One or two young male colleagues in the office tried to make dates with me but I wasn't interested, because Ian and I started to meet regularly in Chester. Our friendship blossomed gradually into real affection, although at first I was reluctant to acknowledge it as such.

"How's the romance going?" Edith asked a few months after our holiday in the Lake District, and I replied cautiously, "It's too young to be a romance - let's just call it a platonic friendship, and as that it's going very well indeed."

In fact, in those days most young folks' conception of romance was more or less within the very limited bounds of Ethel M Dell's novels, in which the hero and heroine plighted their troth with a lingering kiss as the sun sank behind the Himalayas or some equally unlikely surroundings.

After a while I decided that Ian should meet my family, and made plans well in advance, impudently giving precise instructions to everyone at home concerning their appearance and behaviour. He came to Runcorn by train one Saturday afternoon (clad in his immaculate uniform) and I introduced him to them all as they sat sedately in the parlour. Grandma, who'd been shorn of her gingham apron and warned that she mustn't on any account bring out the monkey, remained pathetically silent, and Fred looked sullenly uncomfortable on top of the piano stool and in dangerous proximity to one of the vases of flowers I'd scattered around the room. Dad surprisingly tried hard to be sociable; somehow he discovered that Ian was keen on cricket and they were soon busily discussing Lancashire's chances in the county championship. Mother and Beth coped obligingly with refreshments; Uncle Peter announced loudly that he thought very little of the current Prime Minister and then, to my relief, disappeared fairly quickly.

Early in 1939 Ian was sent to London for a series of refresher courses, and was not able to get any leave at all until the beginning of March. Even then it was to be for a weekend only, so he suggested that we should both go down to his home in Truro. Although I'd have to make my own way there, he felt it would be a pleasant break for us and give me the opportunity of meeting his widowed mother and sister Lucy.

I left Runcorn at half past ten on the Friday morning and arrived at Truro station at a quarter to five. Ian was on the platform to meet me and we took a taxi to his home, a mellow stone house named "Heightside". His mother was grey-haired and expensively simply dressed, and seemed to fit into the genteelly shabby surroundings like a lady to the manor born. Lucy was undeniably attractive, with fairish hair, cut in an artistically casual style, and Ian's dark eyes. She almost completely monopolised the conversation that night, recounting her attempts at joining the Women's Auxiliary Territorial Service.

The next day Ian took me into Truro and after lunch on Sunday he and I walked in blissful solitude for a couple of hours in woods close to "Heightside", stopping from time to time to snatch a quick kiss and say how much we were missing each other. As my train clattered homewards, I thought about the state of affairs which was causing girls like Lucy to enlist for service in the forces. It was difficult to recollect exactly how and when the first threatening clouds had loomed, but rumours of the possibility of a forthcoming war against Germany were definitely around in 1938, when newsreels at the cinemas and photographs and articles in "Picture Post" etc, gave proof of Adolf Hitler's relentless progress through parts of Europe. Prime Minister Chamberlain, with his renowned slogan, "Peace in our time", repudiated the likelihood of any immediate retaliation by the British Government - although it was suggested in some quarters that his caution was due mainly to the fact that we were in no position to offer help to Czechoslovakia, Poland or anyone else at a time when consequent German reprisals would have revealed the current inadequacy of our own Army, Navy, Air Force and war equipment. All the same, the Women's Auxiliary Territorial Service - which Lucy was now joining - had been formed that year. Very few people really believed that we might become involved in open hostilities, but as soon as German atrocities showed signs of spreading, they grumbled that at least some precautionary measures should be taken to ensure our safety. Posters on hoardings stressed the need for able-bodied men and women to train for auxiliary service with the armed forces, and firms started to advertise Anderson shelters for speedy erection in private gardens as protection against possible enemy missiles.

When I got home from Truro that day I found that leaflets advising action to be taken in the event of air raids, gas attacks, evacuation of schoolchildren and so on had been pushed through the letter box at No. 12. They all seemed to be very confusing, especially to Grandma, who pronounced them to be, "a sheer waste of good public money" and said she could think of far better ways of spending it, such as helping poor widows like herself to survive.

During the following weeks a few Anderson shelters were put up in the gardens of some homes in Higher Runcorn and, as in most parts of the country, firefighting practices were organised and gas-masks stockpiled in the town. I shut my eyes to the repugnant possibility of such precautions ever being utilised, and I definitely felt no patriotic urge to enlist for any kind of Forces' service. Ian's time was still divided between courses in London and his Chester HQ: his duties appeared to get more and more time-consuming but he never discussed them with me, and without any qualms on my part at least, we began to make plans with Edith and her boyfriend Trevor for a 1939 June hostelling holiday. After much discussion, we agreed that we should start off by train from Chester and then walk in stages down the Welsh coast from Bangor to Aberystwyth, and inland to Shrewsbury. Trevor made advance bookings at various Youth Hostels en route for us, and we were busy with last-minute lists of items to be carried in our rucksacks when Ian shattered us with the news that his anticipated leave had been cancelled and he was being transferred to Dover on a temporary basis for an indefinite period. I assumed immediately that we should have to call off all the arrangements, but he insisted that it would be a pity for the rest of us to forego our holiday. I could see that Edith and Trevor agreed, and Trevor said he might manage to persuade David Gerrard (who worked with him in the ICI offices in Runcorn and was a keen hosteller) to take Ian's place. David accepted the invitation unhesitatingly, and Ian came to Chester station to see us all off.

We stayed at hostels at Bangor, Llanberis, Lake Cwellyn, Beddgelert, Harlech, Dolgellau (where wolves howled outside the bedroom windows), Towyn and Newtown (in Shropshire).

The longest distance we covered in a single day was 27 miles, and we never once resorted to any form of transport. The weather was marvellous (indeed it was throughout the whole summer of 1939) and my only regret was that Ian hadn't been able to share the enjoyment. Dave (as he'd asked us to call him) had been pleasant company, but he was seven years older than Edith and me and as far as I was concerned just filled an unwelcome gap in our earlier arrangements. A letter from Ian awaited me when I got back to No. 12. Apparently he hadn't received any of my postcards and seemed to be very dissatisfied with life. He wrote that he was unlikely to move back to Chester on a permanent basis until at least the end of September but then, to my great delight, he'd added that he hoped that when he did we'd get married.

# Chapter 16

The next two months (July and August) brought a great deal of upheaval throughout the whole country. Towards the end of August things really seemed to reach a head, and conversation concerning the current state of affairs altered significantly from a previous vague conjecture of, "If we go to war with Germany" to the definite presumption, "As soon as war is declared."

Compared with more industrial and higher populated areas, Cheshire itself was not likely to be classed as of primary importance by the Germans, but both Runcorn and Chester were situated in what could prove to be the route of hostile aircraft heading for the ports of Liverpool and Manchester and of course the big chemical works in the Runcorn, Widnes and Northwich districts and the air base at Sealand, just outside Chester, might also be tempting targets for them.

During the late summer workmen were constructing public air raid shelters hurriedly at various spots in Runcorn, including one between Highfield and Churchfield Terraces, some in the playground at Victoria Road School, and two tunnelled into sandstone in the side of Runcorn Hill. Branches of the Red Cross and St John's Ambulance societies and the Women's Voluntary Service enrolled new members swiftly and started to give training in first-aid and assist with the distribution of gas masks to everyone in the town. Air raid posts were opened up in places obviously chosen for convenience rather than suitability of structure, such as the abandoned shack which had once served as a snack bar alongside the Transporter Bridge. The elderly gent who used to tend the gardens at

"Birchwood" joined a group of air raid wardens operating from a disused stable near to The Grapes Inn in Halton Road. He seemed to consider himself to be of great importance and strutted around with a whistle hanging from a piece of string on his neck, and a rattle hooked to his belt in readiness for alerting us with the news of poisonous gas in our neighbourhood. His enormous tin helmet inscribed ARP in bold letters reached almost down to his eyes and was secured tightly under his receding chin by knotted webbing. It was rumoured that during their nightly vigils he and his mates refreshed themselves periodically by nipping into the pub for a quick pint.

There were even more signs of pre-war activity in Chester. We were accustomed to seeing service outfits due to the proximity of the Army barracks at the Castle, military headquarters on the opposite bank of the Dee, and the RAF base at Sealand, but their numbers grew as men from other parts of the country came to train in the area and looked around for cinemas, pubs and dance halls in which to pass their free time. Camps had been set up a few miles outside the city for refugees who had managed to escape before the Germans completely wiped out their own lands. As elsewhere, air raid shelters were erected speedily throughout the city (including two big underground ones below the Blossoms Hotel at the top of St John Street, and the shopping arcade in Eastgate Row). The windows of our Government Telecommunications building were covered with wire-mesh panels, and emergency regulations concerning procedure for the destruction of confidential information in the event of any necessary evacuation of the premises were circulated urgently around the office.

In the last few days of August it was evident that everything was about to come to a climax and, on 1st September, there was a panic evacuation of schoolchildren and a handful of teachers from Runcorn to Blackpool. Liverpudlians were unpleasantly surprised when all the city lights were switched off that night, and they had their first taste of the black-out restrictions which were to be their lot for the next few years. Historic relics and valuable paintings had already been transferred from the Museum, Walker Art Gallery and so on to comparative safety, and windows of most big shops had been boarded up as a precaution against falling glass and debris.

Early on the morning of Sunday, 3rd September Dad's ear was trumpeted to the radio at No. 12, because in the previous evening's news bulletin the Prime Minister had announced that Britain would declare war on the Germans unless their troops were withdrawn from occupied Poland by 11 am the next day.

I went to Halton Road Church for the morning service as usual; everyone looked very solemn and, at the end of the first hymn, one of the sidesmen walked up to the pulpit and passed a note to the minister, who informed us gravely that the proclamation had indeed been made from Downing Street. Doleful confirmation was written all over Dad's face when I got home, and Grandma was declaring vehemently that, "If Mr Chamberlain had had the sense to clout that Hitler chap with his umbrella a year ago, none of this would be happening today!"

I was, of course, immediately very concerned about Ian. Most people imagined that once war was declared our troops would be sent to France or the Netherlands without delay: I'd tried not to dwell on the fact that his posting to a port convenient for rapid transit across the Channel looked ominous, but now I was desperately afraid that the definite opening up of hostilities might involve his going further afield quite soon.

During that weekend tales of the call-up of Runcorn people who had enlisted previously for auxiliary service with the forces circulated quickly, and several couples were planning hurried weddings at the local Registry Office. I realised that

Edith's Trevor and Dave Gerrard (who had enrolled for voluntary service with an RAF Balloon Barrage contingent when recruitment personnel had visited the ICI offices in Runcorn shortly after our June holiday) might also have been affected. The abrupt disappearance of reservists at once caused some empty chairs in our office, and excepting for a few seniors with specialised technical knowledge and experience, it was likely that most of the remaining males would be liable for conscription sooner or later. On Monday, staff meetings were called hurriedly and we were told that various new aspects of departmental responsibility we'd been made familiar with recently (such as the transmission of air raid warnings via the telephone exchanges which we controlled) were being introduced, and warned that overtime would have to be enforced immediately to cover the duties of departed colleagues.

Everyone was forced in one way or another to adjust to changed conditions. Once the Auxiliaries had been gathered in there was a rush of young male volunteers eager to follow them - some keen to enrol quickly with the forces branch of their own choice rather than be conscripted into one of the others at a later date. In due course Labour Exchanges dealt with enforced enlistment by age group. Men who were too old or unfit for active combat joined the Local Defence Volunteers (later known as the Home Guard); they were sometimes ridiculed (as illustrated in the television programme "Dad's Army"). There were also a few conscientious objectors to active service (known as Conchies), most of whom belonged to peculiar religious sects and were sent to work on farms or in munitions factories.

A number of girls enrolled or were conscripted into women's sections of the Army, Air Force and Navy, or the Land Army. Maureen was one of Runcorn's earliest volunteers for the ATS and had already been despatched to an ack-ack unit on the East coast. Almost at once many were transferred compulsorily from jobs of minor importance to essential work in factories or on the railways and buses, and in our town, into the tanneries, where there was an instant increased demand for leather for the manufacture of boots and belts for Forces personnel.

In the late autumn of 1939 fresh posters appeared on hoardings, some warning us that "Careless talk costs lives", "Walls have ears", and "Look out, there's a spy about"; others to "Make do and mend" and "Dig for victory".

For a short while all the cinemas were closed but they re-opened in Runcorn and Chester once there seemed to be no immediate likelihood of enemy attacks. Pubs stuck to normal opening hours but were almost empty because nobody was keen to risk going out in the dark.

Black-out restrictions were enforced everywhere and ARP wardens paced up and down every night to make sure that no lights were visible. Complying with instructions given on warning leaflets, Beth stuck strips of black adhesive tape in a criss-cross pattern over all the windows of No. 12.

The RAF contingent to which Trevor and Dave were now permanently attached hoisted their barrage balloons over local chemical factories and docks. The balloons were hydrogen-filled, 62ft long and 25ft in diameter and could be flown to an altitude of 5,000ft. They were meant to be a deterrent to low-flying enemy aircraft (which could get entangled in the steel mooring cables) but in rough weather they had to be brought down in case they broke free and drifted away. Most industrial concerns in our district formed their own firewatching and defence squads and erected outsize air raid shelters for the use of employees, and Government offices and public buildings everywhere were protected by stacks of sandbags (creosoted to stave off climatic effects).

A large underground shadow factory was constructed beneath land between the Manchester Ship Canal and the

River Mersey. It was known locally as "the hush-hush place" and like many other factories in the area was camouflaged to look from the air like a stretch of fields and woods. It was rumoured that employees there had to wear special clothing for highly dangerous jobs and were paid by the Ministry of Supply, but otherwise Runcornians had no real knowledge of its intended objective.

Of course both the canals were put to maximum use - barges on the Bridgewater carrying coal and other necessities to the industrial sites, and liners from Atlantic convoys importing foodstuffs into Manchester via the Ship Canal. There were a number of concrete gun emplacements and pillboxes at strategic points such as bridges over the Ship Canal, and stop-planks stored alongside the Bridgewater were multiplied and maintained carefully in case they were needed to hold back water in the event of bomb damage to the banks. Uncle Peter's boat worked almost non-stop, dredging sand from the river for sandbags and transporting grain from Liverpool Docks to storage sheds at Ellesmere Port. As the Transporter stopped running at 11pm (and also during air raids) he often had to walk home from Widnes late at night via the footpath along the iron railway bridge, which was guarded constantly at each end by armed sentries, and he was always challenged at gunpoint with a sentry's, "Halt, who goes there? Friend or foe?" and ordered to produce his identity card for examination by torchlight before he was allowed to cross.

Overtime at the Highfield Tannery was almost incessant, too, (in fact the tannery's weekly capacity, which had initially been 50 hides at the time of its opening in 1888, rose to 7,000 by the end of the war). Dad frowned all the more over the compilation of his "book" because he was required to complete an additional column in it to show reasons for workers' absences, and was infuriated by having to make continual entries for "upset stomach", "bad back" and "looking after two children with measles", and so on against the names of females the firm had recruited into his gang. The little iron gates and railings across the front of Highfield Terrace were requisitioned as part of the national salvage campaign and, with his usual pessimism, he forecast dolefully that the gardens would become a playground for all the dogs in the neighbourhood. An "I wish to inform you" letter to the relevant department in the Town Hall brought forth no sympathy, so he resorted to periods of vigilance behind the parlour curtains and could frequently be seen dashing out through the front door to order intruding animals to move on.

Mother, more harassed than ever by struggling to make both financial ends and rations meet, plodded on with household chores. Beth (who always shied away from any real unpleasantness) continued quietly in her office job but also joined a Help from Home Circle making comforts for servicemen, and seemed to be forever surrounded by shapeless masses of knitting. Fred, who (to our knowledge) had never missed a day off school, surprisingly failed a Conscription Board medical examination due to a kidney weakness. He was kept on as a wheelwright at the Manchester Ship Canal Company's repair yard and enrolled for part-time service in the Home Guard. Understandably, Grandma didn't adjust at all well to wartime conditions and consigned "that Hitler chap" to hell fire regularly for being responsible for Peter's long hours on the boat and a shortage of the provisions she liked to pack into his weekly baskets.

In February 1940 Maureen called to see me, already boasting a stripe on the sleeve of her smart khaki uniform; her lisle stocking seams were meticulously straight and she wore a flashy engagement ring on her left hand. She said she was planning to marry a soldier who in civilian life was a policeman, and I couldn't help wondering whether she'd ever tell him about her shoplifting escapades! I saw Dorothy only rarely, usually in the vicinity of the solicitor's office where she worked as a telephonist. Her prettiness had surprisingly faded quite rapidly - naturally the ringlets had disappeared, but she had also put on quite a lot of weight and (probably due to the huge quantities of sweets she'd consumed as a child) her teeth were already showing distinct signs of decay. In the comfortable security of Ian's love I no longer envied her.

# Chapter 17

For the first few weeks of 1940 I was fully occupied with my job at the office, as by then I'd been put on to duties undertaken previously by a young man who'd decided to join the RAF. The promotion meant that I was able to start saving money at last, with the added incentive of building a nest-egg to contribute towards a home for Ian and me once the war ended.

At the end of March he had another unexpected weekend off duty, and to cut down his travelling we spent two nights at the Henry VIII Hotel in Shrewsbury. The weather was very pleasant and warm enough for us to sit in the park at the side of the river, watching swans and the odd rowing boat go by, and making plans for an autumn wedding. We also looked at engagement rings in shop windows but both felt we should ask Dad's agreement before buying one. All the same, we decided definitely that weekend that we'd get married quietly at Halton Road Church the following September.

As in every other town in the country, Runcornians settled down slowly to what was to them either the bustling activity or tremendous boredom of wartime conditions. Throughout the Spring of 1940, historic fortifications in Chester were revived with modern military equipment and a big extension of communications systems was undertaken. Closure of the city racecourse at the Roodee for the duration of hostilities meant that staff in our office would be deprived of customary time-off for viewing parts of the traditional first-week-of-May events, although juniors were given an hour's leave of absence to watch Princess Mary ( then the Princess Royal) inspect troops at the castle. Edith and Trevor announced their engagement and urged me to consider the prospect of a double wedding, with Dave Gerrard as joint best man. Each week Runcorn newspapers reported happenings concerning local folk away on active service, and I read that Danny White (the CWS scholarship holder who'd done his homework on the stairs) had lost his life when the battleship "Royal Oak" was sunk in a German U-boat attack on Scapa Flow, and one of our old bonfire-pile watchers had been blown to bits during firing practice at an Army site on the South Coast. Another issue published a letter in which Flight Lieutenant Nelson (who as a young lad wore a bow-tie at the Tannery scholarship examination) asked local townspeople to help servicemen by supporting national savings schemes.

Although daylight hours seemed to be lengthening slightly, there was little pleasure in taking solitary walks in what free time I had. Sometimes I tramped for a few miles along the Bridgewater Canal towpath, and noticed that cargoes on the barges were mainly of coal - I supposed the Potteries trade for which some of them had previously carried china clay and crates of finished products was now regarded as an unessential luxury. In spite of the fact that as I'd grown older the age gap between Beth and me appeared less, we hadn't become any closer. Her nervous fits were only spasmodic, but she also suffered with acne quite badly, just when her old schoolfriends were getting married and having first babies. Edith's Trevor and Dave Gerrard helped to keep a barrage balloon afloat near Hale Lighthouse, on the opposite side of the Mersey estuary, where Edith visited them occasionally, laden with home-made goodies. My class of Sunday School scholars shrank perceptibly due to the evacuation, and it was generally appreciated that the annual outings to Frodsham Hill - and also Runcorn's Whit

*River Dee at Chester.*

148

Walks, Carnivals and Wakes Weeks would have to be postponed indefinitely.

I kept Ian's photograph propped against the big jug on Grandma's bedroom wash-stand, and looked at it longingly every day.

Service leave was curtailed drastically in April, and there seemed little hope of his getting any more time off in the foreseeable future. I worried incessantly that he might already be earmarked for taking part in the cross-channel invasion which had been rumoured for some time. Near the end of the month, my fears were confirmed when he rang me at work with the devastating news that he was to start one week's embarkation leave in two days' time. He said he'd be spending the beginning of it with his mother in Truro, and come up to Cheshire for the last three days. He couldn't possibly be accommodated at No. 12, so we arranged to stay at the Stafford Hotel in Chester.

He wasn't at all communicative: professing that he hadn't been told when he'd be leaving Dover nor where he was to be sent, although after he had twice mentioned casually that according to cinema newsreels men of the British Expeditionary Force were currently counter-attacking Germans in the Low Countries, I hazarded a private guess at his probable destination.

I shall never forget those three days. The sun shone every day and we walked for hours along the banks of the Dee, round the old city walls and in Grosvenor Park, where huge clumps of early flowers proved, Ian said, that just as Spring always follows Winter, better times would come for us when the war finished. He bought my engagement ring at Dimmer's Jeweller's shop in the Rows, foregoing Dad's agreement after all. We knew he wouldn't object, though; even Grandma, who on noticing Ian's surname and mine both began with the letter B had warned, "To change the name but not the letter is to change for the worse and not the better," had admitted that she would have expected my choice of a future husband to have been far less satisfactory - and from her that was equivalent to a seal of approval.

So, like lots of other young couples that month, Ian and I made the most of our brief spell together, and before parting tried to assure each other that happier days weren't far away.

In our case, at any rate, they were not to be, because we never met again. Two days after he returned to Dover he was shipped across to Belgium and killed on 15 May during a Luftwaffe assault on the divisional headquarters of the unit to which he'd just been assigned.

# Chapter 18

The news of Ian's death came to me in an urgent letter from Lucy, dated 18th May 1940. It was a handful of sentences which turned my whole life upside down.

At first I just couldn't believe what had happened, and then sank into a sort of dazed numbness in which I had no feeling at all. As the days went slowly by without any letters or 'phone calls from him I gradually began to acknowledge bleakly that Ian was dead - I should never see his smile nor know the warmth of his kisses again; there would be no more walks together beside the Dee or round the walls in Chester, no autumn wedding and no little family house being built for us after the war as we'd planned. All our hopes had dissolved into a funereal pile of ashes: I was left with a bitter anger in which hatred of Germans was uppermost, and was convinced that I should never again be able to murmur, "...as we forgive those who trespass against us" when repeating the Lord's Prayer with the rest of the congregation at Halton Road Church. I wrote a letter of condolence to Ian's mother but received only a brief note from Lucy in reply, together with a couple of letters I'd sent to him while he was at home in Truro.

About an hour after the Prime Minister's declaration of hostilities in 1939, the first air-raid warning of the war had sounded when an unidentified plane was spotted heading towards the South Coast, where people from then on were forced to regard the blare of sirens as customary. There had been a few false alarms in our North Western part of the country during the first winter of the war, but in the spring of 1940

Runcornians became aware of an increasing number of German night attacks on other parts of Merseyside, when the heavy drone of bombers and flashing searchlights over the river were followed by a rumble of anti-aircraft guns, and the glow of fires caused by bombs the planes dropped could later be seen blazing in the distance.

At No. 12 we felt at first that we were in uncomfortable proximity of the raids, and at the start of the night-time activity used to jump out of bed and dress hastily as soon as the sirens wailed their warning, grab the holdall containing belongings Dad considered to warrant essential preservation (including birth certificates, grave deeds, bank books, his RAOB regalia and Uncle Peter's money boxes) and hurry along to the supposed safety of the concrete-topped shelter between Highfield and Churchfield Terraces. The dressing of Grandma often curbed retreat from No. 12 because she used to insist obstinately on donning her corsets, numerous layers of petticoats etc and even the black hat complete with hat-pins before she'd leave the house.

"I'll not be rushed by that Hitler chap and his wicked Nazis!" she declared, with a show of the same stoic determination as Queen Mary, who was reputed to have likewise dressed with her usual attention to detail when she was aroused by sirens at Sandringham in the early hours of the day following the declaration of war. Unfortunately I inflicted what proved to be the final blow to Grandma's dignity in that respect when whilst struggling to help her get into her various garments I pushed both her legs frantically through one of the two openings at the bottom of her calico drawers, and forced her to hurry for shelter in that sorry state. Thereafter she refused to even get out of bed if the sirens sounded during the night, stating firmly, "If my time's come the good Lord will take me, without all that fuss!" and of course we couldn't dash off and leave her - even to the mercy of the good Lord. Sometimes we used to take cover in the pantry under the stairs if the ack-ack fire seemed to be ominously persistent, because it was rumoured that staircases had been left standing after the main structures of the houses had been demolished during London and Liverpool blitzes but, as time passed without real incident in our locality, we started to treat the warnings with complacency, and on hearing them just used to comment that it looked as if Liverpudlians were in for another bad night, and snuggle down in our beds.

One Saturday afternoon later that year a German plane, dashing out of the range of British Hawker Hurricanes after an unsuccessful daylight attack on the docks at Manchester, jettisoned its remaining bombs on to a field near to Warrington, where a church fete had just been opened. Sixteen people were killed and 43 injured (including children), and the tragic event made us realise that despite our recent serenity we might have to face similar danger at any time. There was a brief night raid on Runcorn itself in August 1940, but no resultant loss of life and very little damage. Later the same year a bomb completely demolished a house in the town, and a cottage close to one of the ICI factories was destroyed by a land-mine. On a few other occasions there was slight damage to residential property but all the incidents were obviously merely the result of haphazard attacks, and despite a later discovery that ICI Runcorn was included in the Gestapo's "Arrest List for Great Britain" it did seem that German pilots were miraculously unaware of the vulnerability of the district. Even the bridges over the river appeared to be overlooked.

Most local schoolchildren who had been evacuated to Blackpool returned home fairly quickly as soon as the worst fears of bombing died down (and some because the Government started to enforce contributions towards their upkeep while they were away).

The evening services at Halton Road Church were held in the ground-level Sunday School room, with the windows shrouded by heavy curtains and everything in semi-darkness. They were generally poorly attended and sometimes cancelled altogether.

As more and more men went off to fight, the demand for local Civil Defence volunteers increased. At our Chester office four elderly men were earmarked to deal with any daytime emergencies and a staff rota for the firewatching was set up to safeguard the premises during the night (including Saturdays and Sundays), when one male and two females were scheduled to take over the responsibility. Edith and I paired together for our quota of the duties but our male companions varied, as there were not enough men to allow for any single one of them to make up a regular trio. We were provided with camp beds and bedding in two rooms on the ground floor of the building and toilet facilities were two floors further up, in a cloakroom normally utilised by day staff. Watchers were paid half a crown a night to cover the cost of a snack meal, which we could prepare in the kitchen in the basement. Members of the Red Cross Society trained us in emergency first aid, and ARP personnel demonstrated the use of stirrup-pumps, anti-gas devices and the procedure for putting out incendiary bombs by smothering them with sand. We were each supplied with a tin helmet, specially-equipped gas mask and asbestos-padded gloves. Buckets of sand and water were dotted around the corridors and the very first item on our list of duties for the evening was to check that they were full. Male members of the teams were expected to remain in post in the building throughout all hours outside those normally worked on weekdays by day staff, but in the summer girls didn't firewatch until dusk; after a quick tea in either the kitchen or Hignett's fish-and-chip bar in Frodsham Street, Edith and I used to go to the cinema (to see films like "Mrs Miniver" and other wartime epics) and once we treated ourselves to a live concert at the Odeon featuring Henry Hall and his dance band. Fortunately none of our department's firewatchers were ever called upon to prove their efficiency.

Due to gradual depletion of staff we were asked to do lots of overtime; the journey home was often irksome and, on dark nights when the Luftwaffe was bombarding Liverpool, quite terrifying. The sky was then lit up by flares dropping from enemy planes, and sharp cracks and flashes followed as the anti-aircraft guns at Aston and Ellesmere Port hit out in defence. Sometimes the train halted completely during a raid, and the engine's fire was almost extinguished in case it was spotted by the attackers. One night it must have fizzled out altogether, because a whole hour went by before there was enough steam to start up again, and after another two similar stops I reached Runcorn long after midnight. I could always be certain of a special treat after such infuriating delays though... the supper Mother cooked for me as soon as I got home, whatever the time. It was only a fry-up of left-over-from-dinner potatoes and other vegetables but, piping-hot and smothered in piccalilli, nothing ever tasted nicer.

I used to help eke out the rations at home by having most weekday lunches at the Government-sponsored British Restaurant in Northgate Street in Chester. (There were similar ones in all the cities and most big towns). Choice was limited and you had to queue patiently for counter service, but you could get a generous two-course meal for one shilling and sixpence.

Every Thursday (traditionally the city's market day, when the BR was consequently crowded) Edith and I would ring the changes by going to the Tamil Cafe in St Werburgh Street, where rabbit pie was usually shown as a "special" on the menu that day. On one occasion we were surprised to see a notice hanging on the wall inside, announcing to customers: "Rabbit pie again tomorrow." We hadn't seen the like before and were very amused by the reply from Molly, the waitress, when we questioned her about it.

"Well - there were a lot of Jerries heading for Liverpool on Tuesday night," she explained, "and they say it's an ill wind .... anyway, we get our rabbits from a man who lives out in the country - I suppose he's a poacher really, because he puts down nets to catch them - and he reckons that all the flashing of searchlights and noise from the guns that night terrified the rabbits so much that the poor things nearly went crazy and scuttled off into the woods to get out of the way. Scores of them landed in his nets and he had to make four trips with his wheelbarrow to carry them all home. Judging by the number still hanging out in the backyard here, we'll be having rabbit pie on the menu for several days to come!."

Once or twice Edith invited me to spend a weekend with her; I used to borrow her sister's bicycle and we went for runs to various places outside the city boundary, skirting camps which had been newly set up - some catering for prisoners of war (sent daily to work on farms or in factories) and others accommodating men exiled from European forces who were being given refresher training before attachment to British troops. (A girl in our office volunteered for canteen duties on Sundays at one of the latter camps and ended up with a very long married name composed mainly of s's and z's). There was always something to add interest to our cycle runs; one day we saw a long stream of tanks and armoured vehicles on the road as a throng of servicemen departed from a training site and gave a series of loud wolf whistles as they passed us, and on another, a small group of evacuee children who were billeted in a nearby village and had been sent out to pick rosehips from hedgerows stopped us in our tracks to ask what they looked like - their homes were in Birmingham and they'd never seen any before!

That day Edith and I abandoned the idea of a later visit to our favourite cinema and stayed to help them with their task - after all, scrambling around in the sunshine and topping-up jam jars with rosehips seemed far preferable to watching depressing Pathetone newsreels about further batches of air raids, unsuccessful British counter-attacks on enemy-occupied ports across the channel, and the sinking of more of our ships.

My bitterness over Ian's death subsided gradually into placid disillusionment, and my only real interest was in my job. Dave Gerrard had contacted me when he heard that Ian had been killed, and later kept in touch rather persistently. The balloon barrage contingent was moved away from our neighbourhood and he had transferred to an air station at Mildenhall in Suffolk, where he serviced radio equipment in Lancaster bombers (the machines used in the renowned Dambusters' raid on the Mohne Dam).

In November 1940 enemy attacks flared up again with a vengeance and Merseyside (particularly Liverpool and Bootle) suffered some of the heaviest bombing of the whole war. The raids usually started in the early evening and went on until about midnight, and folk who risked the danger of falling shrapnel to view events from Runcorn Hill said that the city had appeared to be engulfed in huge balls of fire every night. When Mother answered a knock on the door at No. 12 on the morning after an extremely severe raid she was astounded to see her older sister Sara and her husband on the doorstep. A land-mine had wiped out the whole of Suffolk Street in Bootle, where they had lived close to the dockland timber yards, and they had nothing left but the clothes in which they were dressed. They'd come out of an air-raid shelter at daybreak to find that their home was just a pile of bricks and plaster at the bottom of a huge crater and their many other tales of catastrophe and carnage in the area appalled us.

The Salvation Army supplied our evacuees with a bed and somehow we squeezed it into the parlour. They stayed with us for nine weeks and then moved back to Bootle, where a prefabricated bungalow was allotted to them.

Shortly after the outbreak of war there had been development of an airfield complex at Burtonwood, near to Warrington. A large number of planes were stored in hangars, and Nissen huts housed air crews and staff employed in supportive maintenance and supply depots. Following the Japanese attack on their Pacific naval base at Pearl Harbour, the United States entered the war at the end of 1941 and in June 1942 American forces arrived on the site at Burtonwood, and GI helmets became common in nearby streets. Military policemen wore white helmets and were nicknamed "Snowdrops". The Americans were well paid and often passed on cigarettes, chocolate, chewing gum, lipsticks and nylons (all of which, unlike us, they could obtain easily) to civilians in the locality. They invited townspeople to dances and other social events at the site: most of the invitations went to young females and many resulted in romances and marriages (and probably quite a few broken hearts!). Events at Burtonwood were in fact later used as a theme for the film "Yanks". Runcorn girls often went into Warrington by bus; I was never tempted to indulge in the Anglo-American co-operation myself but contemplated that if Maureen hadn't been posted to an ATS unit so far away she would no doubt have been having a whale of a time!

Enemy hostility seemed to die down for a while and there were hardly any raids on Merseyside. One night German planes returning from a solitary attack on Liverpool dropped surplus bombs haphazardly while attempting to dash out of range of pursuing Spitfires, and scored a direct hit on a sanatorium at Barrowmore, near to Chester, but activity in no way compared with the big November 1940 blitz, and Runcornians could remark quite truthfully that at least things were "All quiet on the Western Front".

# Chapter 19

War operations became so widespread and complicated eventually that we were all confused about exactly what was going on and where. Newsreels at the cinemas seemed to relay a perplexing jumble of hostile activity in Italy, North Africa, the Far East and even Russia. D-Day for the counter-invasion of Europe was planned for 5th June 1944 but had to be postponed for a day due to bad weather.

Grandma was extremely puzzled by the unfamiliar names she heard mentioned on the radio, and obviously not at all sure whether it was Mussolini, Eisenhower, Stalin or Montgomery who deserved a fate similar to "that Hitler chap". According to her frequent condemnations they were each in turn responsible for shortages in smoked bacon, Castellan cough mixture and even Peter's long-legged woollen underpants.

As well as publishing details of Runcornians who had been killed in action, local newspapers started to mention any known to have been taken as prisoners of war. Residents of the town "adopted" the escort vessel HMS Flamingo to receive their special interest and support. They organised whist drives, jumble sales and so on with that objective.

I was still working in Chester and, despite continual movement of most Army and RAF personnel, Dave Gerrard remained in Mildenhall (and in fact did so for the rest of his war service). He kept in constant touch and I wasn't exactly surprised when he asked me to marry him.

Edith had already married her Trevor at the Registry Office in Chester, with no fuss at all. I was relieved that I wasn't invited, because in view of the fact that Edith and I had once considered sharing a double wedding I couldn't have faced going alone to theirs. She often warned me that if I didn't get a move on I should be "left on the shelf" and Dave (who was seven years older than me) had apparently started to think on the same lines concerning himself.

I'm afraid I weighed up the pros and cons of his proposal rather unromantically: I certainly didn't want to be a spinster for the rest of my life, and without doubt he and I got on with each other very well. The real reason for my indecision of course was that I couldn't forget the much deeper affection Ian and I had shared, although I knew that hope of that being re-incarnated was as spectral as the advent of a heatwave in Antarctica.

Women civil servants who married during wartime were re-employed in a temporary capacity only, and not eligible for promotion. All the effort I'd put into my job - especially in the last few years - would be wasted if I married. In the end, rather in the manner of tossing a coin, I told Dave I would become engaged to him on condition that we shelved our wedding until the war had ended. He agreed to my terms reluctantly, and we announced our engagement.

Everyone at No. 12 approved wholeheartedly; Grandma instantly tried to get me started on a "bottom drawer" for the collection of pots and pans and the like, and Aunt Emma offered to store them in a spare bedroom for the duration of the war. I accepted the proposals with lukewarm enthusiasm, and oftener than not it was Beth who stood patiently in queues to buy scarce household items which appeared suddenly and very briefly in local shop windows.

Most Government departments were by that time sadly depleted of male staff and, to alleviate the situation, ours announced that female officers with qualification in a technical subject were to be given the opportunity of competing for high-grade posts for which men only had been considered previously. It was possible to obtain such qualification by means of a correspondence course. Contemplating that at least that would relieve my boredom at home, I enrolled for one in Technical Electricity and, after swotting hard for a few months, sat the City and Guilds exam and was awarded a First Class Certificate. Following an interview at our London headquarters I was given a Telecommunications Assistant post in Chester, and felt that at last I'd achieved something really praiseworthy - even though, like Grandma's monkey, I'd toppled downwards a few times in the process!

Once I'd settled in my new job the months flew by and I should have been quite content to continue in those comfortable circumstances for any length of time if Dave hadn't grown impatient about getting married. In the end he got so fed up with my dithering that he threatened to break off our engagement unless I married him at once, so after getting confirmation that I'd be allowed to stay on my new job, I agreed to go ahead with our wedding.

Under wartime conditions few young people aimed at traditional "white" weddings, sometimes due to hurried overseas postings but more often because of clothes rationing. Uncle Peter was adamant that the brown pinstripe he'd bought for Mother's marriage was in good enough shape to wear at mine, and gave me the whole of his year's clothing allowance. I realised later that mothballs advertised themselves very pungently, but I was able to get the turquoise suit I thought would look right on the day and still be useful afterwards.

At that time it was almost impossible to buy wedding presents hitherto regarded as customary. Those we received included seven water sets: I suppose the donors felt they'd given something sizeable, but Aunt Emma was left to store seven jugs and forty two tumblers along with everything else for the duration of the war. Grandma gave us a rolling-pin, Peter subscribed an alarm clock and Maureen brought along a set of carvers which had been a duplicated gift at her own wedding. I should have liked her to be a bridesmaid alongside Beth at mine, but by then she was heavily pregnant. There was a cut-glass vase from Dorothy and as I unwrapped it I thought smugly that I had amazingly out-run her in the matrimonial stakes, even despite my set-back over Ian.

On the morning of my wedding day I woke up very early and for a while lay listening to Grandma's gentle snores.

"Keep an eye on that clock on the wash-stand tomorrow morning, and wake me up so that I can put the cream on top of the trifle as soon as the milkman's been!" she'd ordered as she was clambering laboriously into bed the night before.

I reflected sadly that, although she'd insisted on supervising the wedding breakfast spread, she seemed to be lapsing fast into real senility. I couldn't imagine her ever being relegated to a wheelchair or bed pans, but before it was too late I must ask her whether she reckoned my monkey had laid itself to rest finally at the top or bottom of its stick.

Beth slumbered on beside me, now and then twitching her head (plastered with spiked curlers in readiness for the big occasion) into a more comfortable position on the pillow. At least I hoped that was why, because it would be dreadful if it meant instead that she was in for one of her nervous spasms!

I checked the time: it still showed up only dimly on the little clock because the black-out curtains still covered the bedroom window, but through a chink of light where they didn't quite meet I could see that at any rate dawn had broken. For some reason I suddenly recollected my crayoned drawing which the Art master had hung on the wall at the Grammar School years ago, and its poetic caption:

"I remember, I remember
 The house where I was born;
 The little window where the sun
 Came creeping in at morn..."

Many narrow boats had travelled along the Bridgewater Canal in front of No. 12 and much water had passed under Runcorn's bridges since then. The sun had shone through the bedroom window often, and I hoped that just now it was indeed just creeping out from behind the tannery chimneys and, before setting again, would give credence to one of Grandma's many quotations - "Happy the bride the sun shines on!"

I jumped out of bed and drew back the curtains.

Clouds driven relentlessly by a high wind were scudding across the sombre sky. It was pouring with rain and looked as though it would never stop.

# Epilogue

In spite of the weather's dismal contribution to our wedding day, Dave and I had 37 years of great happiness together afterwards. Towards the end of the first four of them our son Robert Ian was born.

The war in Europe had ended on 7th May 1945 (VE Day) and, although hostilities still trickled on in the Far East, Dave was demobilised from the RAF in September that year and returned immediately to his job with ICI. I stayed on at the office in Chester until a few months before Robert's birth.

It now seems incredible that great-grandfather Webster's headstone has weathered so many years. During the last four decades Dave, Mother and Dad, Beth, Fred, Grandma and Uncle Peter have all passed away - and also every former member of the original Mason Street household. Grandma's birthday parties continued until she was 87 and Uncle Peter earned top marks for longevity in the family by living to the ripe old age of 91 and thereby confirming one of his favourite sayings that, "Hard work never hurt anybody."

Both Maureen and Dorothy moved away from Runcorn long ago and we have lost touch with each other altogether, but I often visit Edith and Trevor and their two grown-up children in Chester - a city which has managed fortunately to retain much of its ancient heritage and where I always glance nostalgically at the present optician's shop in St Werburgh Street which at one time was filled with the appetising aroma of the Tamil Cafe's rabbit pies, and at the doorway of a small modern store, which used to lead into Quaintways tea-rooms, where Ian and I had sheltered on rainy days and held hands under the little tables.

The war left scars everywhere, of course. As soon as it ended people tried to pick up the threads of a normal existence once more, but some human remnants of the hostilities were sadly never able to really enjoy life again - especially the maimed, and young girls who had lost loved ones but for whom no Dave had come along.

In the ensuing years Runcorn changed a lot.

Trade at the tanneries first started to decline in the 1950s when cheaper substitutes for leather came onto the market, and every single one of the local firms closed down eventually.

The number of ships passing up the Manchester Ship Canal fell significantly once the ports of Manchester and Liverpool became less busy, and paths along the banks on which townspeople once paraded in their summer finery were soon overgrown with weeds and the spreading tendrils of blackberry bushes.

Once Midland potteries began to favour faster road transport as the means of carrying materials into their factories and finished goods out of them, the Bridgewater was utilised almost solely for pleasure purposes (maximum speed 4 mph). Its hump-backed bridges were well-maintained but usually crossed only by the odd fisherman, or straying children and dogs. The slow clip-clop of cart horses faded away, because new owners preferred to propel the narrow boats by modern methods. The old resident barge families became a forgotten race.

Business deteriorated at the docks where great-grandfather Webster's schooner once moored, and after a few years those in Widnes from which Uncle Peter set sail emptied completely.

Of all the old trading concerns which stimulated the area previously, only the chemical industry continued to expand and prosper.

The railway bridge over the Mersey between Runcorn and Widnes was in constant use and inter-city expresses and goods conveyors laden with vehicles produced at the immense Ford factory at nearby Halewood could be seen whizzing across it at frequent intervals, but the Transporter Bridge eventually failed to cope with local requirements and was demolished in 1961. In the year of its demise, however, a new construction of single steel arch design and dual carriageway, running parallel with the railway bridge, was opened by Princess Alexandra of Kent. Before long the amount of traffic passing over it indicated the need for consideration of its extension or maybe the erection of an additional crossing.

With the closure of so many works' premises and the disappearance of familiar landmarks, Runcorn declined slowly into a ghost of its previous bustling activity and prosperity. In April 1964, however, it rose like a Phoenix from the ashes when it was designated to become one of the country's New Towns, with the objective of increasing the number of its inhabitants from about 28,500 on that date to 100,000 by the end of the century, accommodating an overspill population from the Liverpool area and attracting new industry to cater for their employment.

The New Town planners divided the 7,500 acres of land allotted to them into numerous neighbourhood units, each with its own group of shops and various other services and linked together by a public transport route. Huge blocks of flats, housing estates, schools, churches, parks and playing fields have since been dotted around, and a hospital, second railway station, several public buildings and a covered-in main shopping centre with multi-deck car parking facilities have also been

*Runcorn New Town.*

constructed. Intervening areas have been landscaped very pleasantly. Big industrial estates, advertised by television as ideal sites for setting up fresh industry in "The Nation's Most Central Location" now edge the district. Many of the older buildings in the town were mowed down to make way for the extra bus routes and some others have been included in improvement or renewal schemes.

Highfield Terrace and the Tannery buildings are no more. The land where they stood, together with the waste ground which accommodated our bonfires and concrete air-raid shelter, and the field from which I made my first aeroplane trip have been amalgamated to form industrial lots, housing hangar-like single storey pre-fabricated factories. Along with others, Halton Road Church was demolished some time ago, and most of the little shops where, after considerable deliberation, Maureen and I used to spend our weekly pocket money are boarded-up. If Dad were still alive I am quite sure he would be furiously penning, "I wish to inform you..." letters to appropriate authorities.

Mill Brow School is now a Pentecostal Church and the former Grammar School a College of Further Education. Victoria Road School (to me the best-loved dinosaur of Runcorn's educational past and which provided Robert with a primary education leading ultimately to a place at Oxford University) has had a tremendous face-lift and continues to function as efficiently as ever. When HRH Princess Margaret visited it for the celebration of its centenary in 1986, current-day pupils dressed in appropriate costumes demonstrated chalking on slates and embroidering samplers which my mother and her sisters would have engaged in there in its early years. There are several new Comprehensive schools in the district, and adult education is also well catered for.

Citizens' money has been invested wisely in the improvement of social services and community amenities, but unhappily Runcorn has also been subjected to the hooliganism which seems to be prevalent throughout the country. Twenty seven headstones in one of the cemeteries were smashed recently by drunken louts, and although the window I sketched on the site of the 11th century Halton Castle for the Eisteddfod competition had survived continual blasting during the Civil War, stonework surrounding it has now been vandalised to such an extent that scarcely a fragment remains. Hopefully a renovation package which is planned for our town's most prominent and historic landmark may be able to restore some of the castle's former glory.

The combined Old and New Towns are administered by the Halton Borough Council, and remaining spare acres within its boundaries no doubt will be used up in due course to provide further accommodation sites and cultural projects to cater for the population target of 100,000.

Like a stone dropped into a stagnating pond, New Town developers started a ripple of progress here in 1964 which is still spreading outwards.

The old order changeth, giving place to new.